Ecclesiastical Laurels

or Abbot de T***'s Campaigns
with the Triumph of the Nuns, &c.

Attributed to

Jacques Rochette de la Morlière

Translated By Richard Robinson

Sunny Lou Publishing Company
Portland, Oregon, USA
http://www.sunnyloupublishing.com

Second Edition: January 6, 2024
Revised and Corrected: January 4, 2024
Original Publication Date: December 25, 2020

ISBN: 978-1-955392-48-8

* * *

This translation from French is based on the 2nd edition, "corrected and augmented," from 1748, of *les Lauriers ecclésiastiques, ou Campagnes de l'abbé de T***, avec le Triomphe des religieuses, &c.*, published by "the regular printshop of the clergy at Luxuropolis."

Table of Contents

The Ecclesiastical Laurels

Militat omnis amans, & habet sua castra Cupido.[1] – Ovid, *Amor*. Lib. I

IMPORTANT NOTICE, which the reader is advised not to skip over

A publisher avid for praise and thanks would not at all so easily renounce the rights that he might think were his due, and he would emphatically insist that the trouble taken and the research employed to make available so rare a manuscript should be taken into consideration; as for me, I will confess ingenuously that, without priding myself on ill-placed modesty, I believe in all surety that I can rely on connoisseurs to rouse themselves and appreciate justly my vigils and labors; so, without entering into the details as to how this singular work came into my hands, I would say simply that Monsieur the Abbot de T***'s modesty was one of the greatest obstacles I had to surmount in order to be able to communicate to the public a morsel so worthy of its attention; little moved by a reputation he so justly deserved to enjoy, it was after only the most lively discussions that he decided to confess to exploits that he had wanted absolutely to bury the memory of; finally he let himself be won

---

[1]Militat... Cupido: Latin for "Every lover wages battle, & Cupid holds his castle." Ovid, *Amores*, Book I.

over, and I give his manuscript to the public without changing so much as a single syllable; all that remains is that I should warn this same public that if this book should have the good fortune to please, this edition will doubtless be the last, whereas if it should displease to a certain degree, we will not fail to make more copies of it because there is something delicious about seeing frowns and knitted eyebrows... & besides, the more people who manifest ill humor and disquietude over it, the more easily I am persuaded that the portraits and events contained herein are not too distant from verisimilitude and the truth.

Part One: A Coming of Age

I will satisfy you, my dear marquis; you want an exact account of my mischievous behaviors from the moment I came into the world, & of the serious denouement that will soon put an end to them all: in the midst of the successes of a brilliant campaign and an ample harvest of laurels, you imagine there are others that can be snatched with less trouble, & whose less-glorious fruits perhaps have more real and more satisfying sweetness; you believe finally that love can take the place of everything in life: ah! who more than I should want to support that system? It is what has always made my happiness; because of it, I arrive now at the happiest days of my life: and down what road has it led me? how many flowers have I smelled and plucked along my way! No, I have never known its troubles, it has never exercised its power over me except by the continuous and indescribable pleasures it has intoxicated me with. I owe it so much gratitude for so many benefits, and how better can I repay it than by publishing the favors it has heaped on me, the charms it distributed in the early years of my life.

As for the rest of it, my dear friend, I hope you will look beyond its lack of style owing to my naïvety: I have never been an author, and besides, I am writing to a military man; there, I think, those are enough excuses: facts, verve, that is all you have the right to expect from me. But someone will say to me, "not everyone is so easily pleased"; well, here's my response: those kinds of people should not read me; I can quite easily do without their approval, as well as their yawns and their criticism; & I will be amply recompensed by the physical & moral certitude that I have – to be read, commented on, approved, decried, and praised by my dear fellow abbots, useless illustrious fellows, eternal directors of *ruelles*;[2] as well as by all the amiable consciences of people under their charge who are constantly breaking out in rage against the *little pamphlets, who have no idea that one can amuse oneself in things of similar wretchedness,* who however, like them, read nothing else, & who have their own good reasons for it.

Besides, why would I look for justifications or pretexts: you're in the army, where one is obliged to amuse oneself with anything at certain moments; I am presently in a similar situation in Paris: I have nothing to look forward to for several days now except an atrocious solitude, on account of the temporary absence of all I hold most dear. You want me to write to you, to lift your listless spirits; I will not assume the sublime tone of the fastidious Roman in order to trace out for you my adventures, which are for the most part too enjoyable to be susceptible to a serious tone or a starchy bearing; you won't be up for ten or twelve pages of gushy feelings, which I cannot in good conscience grace you with, & I do this not only to honor the profession, but also to render homage to

---

[2]*ruelle*: the space between the bed and the wall.

the truth of my story, which ends with a dignity that neither you nor I were expecting surely, & which my beginnings did not seem to promise me necessarily.

My, what an admirable exordium you might say to me, & I can see in advance that it will be heart-warming for anyone who examines me with sangfroid to see that by seriously asserting that I am not an author, nor a writer, nor a novelist, I assume, without realizing it, all the useless gradations & bothersome regularities of those same gentlemen. What a delicious satisfaction for a gruff critic to see me laying a trap for myself which I thought I could avoid by pointing it out & by being able to say with a bitterly caustic tone, "Eh, yes, it's still a pamphlet like the others," to then look with arrogant distraction at the first and last pages & to exclaim, "Oh, my goodness, I'm not too fond of this! it really is rather boring." And then what, my dear marquis? Let's unleash our ogre, that he might destroy humankind as he pleases: the judgments that apply only to a type of work in general & that are then applied to each one of them in particular, without deigning to examine if they merit an exception, are more risible and more absurd than redoubtable; in fact, I am exactly in the same boat as you are, & all reasonable folk do the same, & for what it's worth, I sovereignly despise them: with that out of the way, I begin my story.

I will spare you a long genealogy of my family, a taking stock of its possessions, & the responsibilities & dignities by which my ancestors distinguished themselves: you know me well enough to have no need of those clarifications, which in any case are really useless for explaining some of the youthful escapades I need to recount; & I have more than one reason for not wishing to further satisfy anyone's curiosity on that score.

You know as well as I do that I was born in Paris, & the rank my family holds there; & you are not unaware that we moved there, & that with all our property being situated in the province of *** from which we originated, & where my ancestors have always kept their residence, the laws of that province, as well as some other extremely unfavorable laws for cadets, leave precious little hope for me as far as regards my family's property; I knew almost from the moment I entered the world that I had an older brother who would one day become a great lord, & at the same time I was instructed on the strict limits that the laws placed on my fortune, & of the necessity I would be in to augment it, either by my ability, or by my ingenuity, or by my flexibility. However disagreeable these ideas were, the indispensable necessity to adopt them and adapt myself to them made them less and less hard for me; without realizing it, I got used to the prospect of mediocrity, which made this yoke more bearable. You knew my brother, you were his friend, & you won't be surprised when I tell you that the happy breadth of his character and his natural disposition, the tender & exquisite friendship that was established between us, at an age when men don't even recognize the name for it, all that, I say, contributed in large part to making me find my lot happier.

We did our studies at the college of ***, I was already in my twelfth year, and my brother was in his fifteenth, before there was even a question of the decisions that would be made in our regard; however because, between the two of us, I was the one whose future was more uncertain, & by consequence more difficult to decide, I was the one taken into consideration first: my brother's career was quite simple, given his birth & his great possessions, the path of public service was the only one he could choose, besides it was what my family had always followed; but feelings were far from united when it came to my future: I was bound to be poor, & it was a question of trying to make me rich, no matter what it cost, or whom; my father brought together a large *committee*, and every one of my relatives in Paris was invited: those who figured among the nobility of the robe were only there to swell the ranks, I was neither rich enough nor poor enough to be one among them, so all the debate for and against was taken up by five or six old military men, my great uncles, or my great cousins, all so laden with the ruins or the honors of war, which taken altogether could not have been sufficient to scrape together one marble bust in its entirety, & who, so as not to bury their madness with them, argued over me like a spoil of war with another certain relative from Prémontré who was in possession of a decent quantity of priories, & who had a chubby face that pleaded furiously in his favor; my dear relatives the officers combatted the soundness of his reasonings by all sorts of sophism & with the profession's most advantageous exposition of brilliant falsehoods, by which they themselves had been blinded formerly: whereupon the stout Prémontré responded to them with a thundering and victorious voice: "Look at me, my dear cousins, examine me and be destroyed; compare your disabled bodies to my stoutness & to the perfection of my existence; the deprivations, the fatigues, & the hazards of your life, with the peaceable and happy tranquility of my own; bewail your error, and the loss of irreparable time, but don't try to make a victim of someone whom I want to lead into safe harbor: the soundness of his arguments did not go unnoticed by my father, but as he had certain prejudices tied to his birth, & which there exist good reasons to maintain and augment in us everyday, I don't know what would have been the Synod's decision if my uncle the Bishop of N*** hadn't joined into the thick of the dispute: his presence put an end to the debate, as soon as he knew what it was about, as soon as he had given himself some time to take in what the victorious Prémontré's reasonings had alleged with triumphant attitude; when he took up his position with passion, my fate was instantly decided. His Greatness arranged that I be tonsured immediately, & that I be put into a position moreover to receive an abundance of goods and favors, with which the Church always recompenses its beloved children, & by which they are made assuredly worthy by observing to the letter the respectable inutility of the kind of life imposed on them.

I was enrolled then among these pious idlers, and instead of Knight one called me, from then on, the Abbot de T***; it was not at first without some

repugnance that I fell in line with my uncle's vocation, but from the moment I was one of his, he took
hold of me with an authority that the miter and its opulence give, & which my father did not dare resist; he
knew so well how to represent to me the solidity of
the advantages attached to his state, & the ease with
which one could make it compatible with all the pleasures in life, which, little by little, I began to open my
eyes to; I recognized in effect that the surest and most
prudent position in life was to impress men, & to live
at the expense of their credulity and good faith. I had
not yet seen any of the abbots except my preceptor, &
by a miracle he turned out to be a wise and honest
man; he was an old Irish priest, tough like a Theban
anchorite, filthy and disgusting in proportion to the
devotion he practiced, bristling with scruples, prejudices, and syllogisms, upright and sincere otherwise,
but whose exterior was not suitable for giving me a
taste for the clergy. I was at that time far from imagining there was in the world a kind of amphibious animal whose ranks I should swell one day; I was ignorant that one gave the name abbot to these tonsured
apes, these privileged street performers, equally suited for ecclesiastical farces & scenes of worldly circle
societies, pagodas consecrated by humankind's stupidity, ignorant of exactly everything, & well-posi-
tioned to profess themselves as all-knowledgeable,
charming pompous buffoons, authorized to decide everything impudently on the approval of some *CHAT-
TERBOXES*, all as amiable & as sottish as they were:
I was ignorant at the time as to their existence and the
possibility of their being; but I didn't rest for long in

so reprehensible an error, I had the occasion to see some of them at my Uncle's place, who passed for the elite among their genre, & in no time at all I took a lot of pleasure in the manners of these gentlemen; by the grace of a dose of impudence & fatuity which young people are always liberally endowed with, I could soon flatter myself as following advantageously in their footsteps & even leaving the greater part of them behind me.

After I had finished my studies, my uncle had me move to a place closer to him & made me study at the Sorbonne: because today it is a saddle for every horse and absolutely necessary that the same cap be pulled down over the ears of a large number of sots who would be quite beside themselves without it, I studied then, but, to be honest, without taking much pleasure in some things – in principle because they began to extort a tyrannical assent from me, which was absolutely contrary to my reasoning: I had already acquired certain notions on matters that appeared to me infinitely more interesting and more tied to nature than all the pompous jibber-jabber they exasperated me with every day. My uncle was one of those high-society prelates who readily relied on the care of his flock, on the care of a Grand Vicar who for his own part was perfectly fine with my uncle's absence: he very seldom visited his bishopric, the country air was so contrary to him! His Greatness, my uncle, had such a delicate stomach! that he was obliged by an incommodious diet to spend his entire life in Paris, to take thermal waters, & to try to preserve his health by all the means available to a tranquil and devoutly comfortable life; his doctor prescribed theatrical plays, a table served with very nourishing dishes, & enjoined him to receive company capable of dissipating certain accesses of black bile that could have imperiled the precious days of his Excellency: he submitted to it all with a resignation that one could only admire, & I was not put out, all things considered, with these prescriptions: some very charming ladies visited him; I devoured every single one of them with my eyes: the diamonds, the rouge, a neck or a leg however so seldom uncovered, caused me indescribable shivers, & as I noticed my dear uncle's eyes sometimes caught by the same objects, & which seemed to me at the time to be very unapostolic, I felt encouraged by so great an example, & prepared one day to become one of the greatest personages of holy legend.

Among the people who came most often to visit my uncle, the Marchioness de B*** was one who caught my eye the most, & I felt myself particularly attracted to her: her charms hadn't escaped me at all, but at the same time I made, due to my penetration, another discovery that didn't help much to moderate my glances and my overzealous attentions: it seemed to me that monseigneur my uncle paid at least as much attention to her as his dear nephew did, & as interested parties in these sorts of matter never fail to notice, I thought I perceived, through the most careful conduct that could be observed by a woman with as much worldliness and experience as the marchioness had, that his Greatness's overzealousness was not received by her in such fashion as to make him lose hope; I was never able in what followed to procure for myself enough information as to know just what their relationship was, nor to what point it had gotten; all that I will add here in justification of the marchioness is that my uncle was, & is still today, quite well endowed with the advantages of wit and figure to merit the attention of whomsoever a woman it might be; & besides, it is well known *that the miter sits well on a furrowed brow*; be that as it may, he wasn't more than forty years old, and he was an extremely handsome man: throw in that leisurely attitude of his, that precious color attached to his state, which gave him the true face of a Seraphim. It will be easy to be persuaded that if, in the adventure that follows, my uncle got the short end of the stick, this was owing more to that fund of frivolity that exists in human nature, which in these sorts of occasion makes the nephews always trip up the uncles, than some other real advantage that ought naturally to have allowed me to gain the upper hand over him.

As for the marchioness, she was a real episcopal piece of tail, an archangel, one of the elect: beautiful as the morning, she was artless and unaffected, twenty-six or twenty-seven years old, enjoying a very large income, & unhampered by her immensely stupid and immensely inconvenient husband, free to make use of all her rights & to enjoy all the pleasures that were hers by birth, & that because of the happy caprice of M. her spouse who spent the greater part of the year on his lands playing lord of the parish, filling the hills and dales with the sound of his dogs and horses: a man of quality for all that, & quite pleased that one should know it, having his genealogical tree displayed in his dining room, & his coat of arms affixed beneath the chateau's eaves; a court case against his curate for honorary rights; disagreements and quarrels with his neighbors because of the hunt; and finally all the inseparable accoutrements of a country gentleman.

Nice digression! you will say to me, as if not everyone is familiar with that type of animal there, & as if it were necessary to draw so annoying a portrait: oh well, accursed critic, pardon me my asides, or stop reading me altogether; I tell you as a friend that, given I am not at all disposed to watching myself, nor to containing myself, you will need, for what lies ahead, a much more obstinate patience to endure a thousand times more of the same.

Back to the marchioness; I saw her every day, and how would that have been possible if I had not been born so fond of or – to speak more accurately – so inclined to women; I would have remained insensible to so many charms: the familiarity she enjoyed in my uncle's house had given me the right to court her at hers: M. the Bishop, the best man in the world moreover, and the least jealous, led me there himself, & seemed to take responsibility for all the little acts of kindness she showered me with; the marchioness for her part, in response to his intentions, received me with a freedom and with a casualness that she decorated by a certain little gentle superiority, which she imagined herself to possess by virtue of her being ten years older than M. the student who was eighteen; it was MY LITTLE PUPIL, MY LITTLE ABBOT, and a thousand other diminutives, that were hung on me while she blushed a little, which had the same effect on me, & which caused a strange emotion in all my little person. I profited pleasurably by every moment that my uncle didn't have his eyes fixed on her, by passionately fixing my own on her: when I think about it now, there must have been something very agreeable in those looks of mine; I had a half-holy, half-profane appearance about me, which must have been quite delightful for a third person, & the consuming fire in my looks tempered by a certain varnish of hypocrisy and wickedness, attached to the blasted robe that I wore, must have seemed like day and night, in a word a very curious contrast.

But I also had a lot of things working in my favor on that occasion! I was young, – you remember the face I had at the time, my dear marquis; I had certain eyes that spoke volumes, and extremely beautiful, thick blond hair; yes, beautiful hair, & lest anyone be mistaken, that had its effect, & it didn't take long before I realized that these bagatelles were sometimes the object of the marchioness' attention; I often caught her looking me over with her big blue eyes full of admirable beauty, & those eyes, for all I could tell, weren't expressing an invincible resistance either; as for M. the Abbot, you can be sure that he made the most of those amorous glances, however novice he may have been at the time; & despite the general system that few women could resist the fixed stare of a grey monk[3] or a military man, I would respond that none of these two comes close to the glance of a seminarist or a student of the Sorbonne, whose uncle is a bishop, & an uncle such as I had.

However, despite all the assiduousness of my amorous glances & the discoveries I thought to have made regarding my beautiful marchioness' dispositions, in good faith I can't say what would have happened & how I might have brought an end to a like enterprise; sottishness is a faithful companion of young men in a first love affair, & because their natural impudence & the perversion they are gifted with are not strong enough to make them surmount it, one must judge from this to what degree the prejudices of their age impose on them & make them have the ridiculous respect that they do for women, the majority of whom are quite far from being happy with so sterile a sentiment; after all, these are the stages all young men must necessarily pass through, & as too often happens they correct the fault by going too far in the opposite direction.

But finally it was fated that she would take my first fruits, & even that she would be responsible for certain preliminaries, that she saw clearly it was no longer possible to abandon me to my penetration;[4] I had guessed correctly when I imagined that I pleased

---

[3]grey monk: possibly a reference to the "Grey Monks," because of the color of their habits, that is, the monks belonging to the Tironensian Order.

[4]penetration: a military term referring to a frontal attack or breach of the enemy line.

her; our feelings for one another had been born at about the same time and in the same way, but they were much more developed in her by experience, practice, and a thousand other things finally that I lacked, & that made me advance trembling on a path that she was running along at top speed: she took it upon herself then to drop me some hints that were a little less equivocal as to her good intentions, & M. the Abbot who was waiting for nothing else, & who through his scholastic naïvety was not made to be one of the less advantaged in this world, didn't mortify her by not picking up on them; I guessed her intent promptly, & I didn't delay in answering her with both passion and gratitude, which the most accomplished little master could have prided himself on, but which he would not perhaps have had it in his power to imitate quite exactly on all points; we were already at sweet nothings & holding hands, & because I had clearly perceived that the marchioness was the favorite sultana in Monseigneur's seraglio, I felt myself all the more obliged to use all the care and consideration needed in so delicate a situation; for her part, she imitated my discretion, & although she found the means to pay me a thousand flattering attentions, to do me a thousand fine things that I would have been quite incapable of doing for her, for want of practice and experience, it was easy for me to see that she was waiting for a more favorable opportunity & that she was prepared to go to any length rather than lose it by some inconsiderate act.

The opportunity didn't take long to present itself: Monseigneur, following his doctor's orders, had leased a stunningly beautiful house in the countryside of N***, where he went regularly in the springtime to take the waters & to take care of his overworked chest by something other than fasts and abstinences; in order to conform exactly, on all points, to his Aesculapius' advice; he had invited a select company of individuals who could assist him in getting over his melancholy; one can imagine quite well that the marchioness was not left behind, & M. the Doctor in Philosophy of the Sorbonne felt the time was right to play hooky from school for six weeks, to also take a break from his work. My uncle was accommodating on that score, he even remembered doing something similar when he was a student, & I made him complicit without his knowing it, & more easily than I would have dared to hope for, in the little projects I had arranged for the relaxation of my mind.

We set out then, all of us, in an extremely joyous mood & in very good health, including his Greatness, who never appeared more sanguine in the face except when he was on the verge of taking some cure: I saw a gleaming look of joy and serenity on the marchioness' face, which I had never seen before, her physiognomy was unlike anything I had noticed in Paris & the way she behaved towards me were both telltale signs of the change I had noticed in all her person. I was superabundantly encouraged by her conduct, which seemed necessarily to lead to the objective of all my desires: truth be told, several short disappearances by the marchioness and my uncle, in the first week or so of our being in the country, didn't escape me, but I didn't pay too close attention to them either; besides, the prelate appeared enormously old to me: a forty-year-old man, I said to myself, is too decrepit to be bothered with the things of this world: foolish as I was, I didn't know then that a soutane and a *rochet* are worth all the fountains of youth, & that the zeal of servants of the Church is, on that occasion, as on all others, much greater than that of feeble men of society.

Whenever I walked in on the marchioness during one of those tête-à-têtes, I saw only a look of embarrassment and alteration on her face: at first I hadn't paid too close attention; but finally without really knowing why, I was seized in all my being suddenly by a change that was easy to perceive: I soon recognized even that the marchioness had noticed my changed state of mind, & that she was not insensible to it; from one day to the next I appeared more distracted and ill-humored. My uncle imagined that boredom had gripped me, & that I was tormented by the desire to continue my theological studies; he offered to have me return to Paris, but I parried the attack by pretexting a complication in my health: this was an important article in the profession I had embraced, it saved me from what I feared; there was no longer any question of hiding a thing of such importance or which put me in a situation of falling short in the most essential duties of my profession, in which one took an oath never to be ill, unless it were due to too much grease and corpulence, an oath that my colleagues keep so religiously, which one so seldom sees among those who can reconcile themselves to breaking it.

I often walked off my reveries in an extremely vast park that lay adjacent to the house where we were staying; because hot weather was approaching, I chose mornings for my walks: I employed a time of day when our ladies were not visible. One day as I was returning at the usual hour, right around meal time, I saw the beautiful marchioness appear at the window; immediately she withdrew & closed it brusquely; I was so far away that I was unable to be sure whether she had seen me or not, and I could not decide if my appearance had occasioned so prompt a retreat; I returned to the house with a thousand thoughts knocking about in my head, & which I didn't dare, nor was able, to sort out; I paid close attention to the marchioness' behavior towards me, & I could not detect the least evidence of my conjectures: same welcome, same glances, same signs of intelligence, but nothing else: in the end, I didn't know what Saint to turn to, nor how to behave with so indefinable a woman, when I heard her two days later complaining of some minor indisposition: to reiterated questions that someone had put to her to better understand the type of illness she was suffering from, she responded like a person who was reluctant to be pressured, that she could attribute it only to the infrequency with which she had taken her doctor's advice, which turned out to be morning baths at the end of spring and at the beginning of autumn; just what she anticipated, happened: she suffered all the reproaches & entreaties common in such cases, which she received with all the requisite simpering airs to persuade everyone of her repugnance; her facial expression and her bearing belied it so strongly that I was confounded, & I couldn't figure her out yet; finally my very dear uncle came to the aid of my stupidity; he assumed the subdued tone of a prelate and a superior to tell her that her conduct was beneath her, that she was acting like a child to the point that it was unsupportable, & he finished by ordering her to obey her doctor & to go every morning to her bathhouse, which was in the park; everyone chimed in, to assure her that they were willing to run the risks that Actaeon did, to penetrate her asylum, & a thousand other vapid comments of this nature, until she gave in, after much resistance however, but not nearly as much as I would have needed to be convinced; oh! for on this occasion M. the Doctor of Philosophy of the Sorbonne opened his eyes: "Yep," I said to myself, "she saw me; she had withdrawn from the window, she knows about my walks in the park, & she will take her prescribed baths in consequence; she wouldn't be trying to swap the nephew for the uncle, would she? if that's the case, she's on, – the opportunity is too perfect; no one would see me tripping over my robe by mistake, taking over where a prelate left off! a simple sub-deacon! there isn't a more beautiful opportunity to enter into the world of high society!"

Such were the reflections and arrangements I made *in petto*;[5] it wasn't the worst rationalization I had ever made since I had started rubbing elbows with this learned group; the consequences were infallible, given the disposition of the individuals in-

---

[5] *in petto*: Italian for "in my heart" or "in my mind."

volved: also, I didn't hesitate to see them justified by the event. I was waiting impatiently for the appointed day when my beautiful goddess began her prescribed regimen; it didn't take long, & as I hadn't made any attempt to discontinue my morning walks, which I maintained were necessary to stay fit, I had the satisfaction of seeing her walk along the path toward the bathhouse in the freshness of the morning: I waited in ambush in a bower, from which it was easy for me to examine her at my ease, & without fear of being discovered; Gods, what charms! yes, my dear marquis, I am at a loss for words to describe what I felt on seeing her; she walked with a negligent and languorous step, in a most beautiful Persian full-length negligee, allowing me to discover the beauty of her waist, the perfect delicacy of her feet, & the shape of her calves which were enough to take one's breath away: with a short muslin cape wrapped around her shoulders negligently, concealing a portion of her admirable bosom, but offering from what remained enough to enflame me with desires; she passed rather close by, so that I could see her eyes, which I imagined to be wet, the certain indication of a secret melancholy, the cause of which I was burning to discover; however, my timidity gaining mastery over me at the same moment, I contented myself with following her & devouring her with my eyes, when I saw her veer off onto the path that led to the baths: I walked around the bathhouse a thousand times without once mustering enough courage to enter, nor even to let myself be seen: finally she exited after the prescribed time & took the walkway back to the chateau; I saw her pass, she had a much sadder look on her face than in the morning. I went back to the chateau a little while later, and I presented myself at her door which was locked; & when the time came for the company of guests to reassemble, she never deigned to cast a glance at me; & if she spoke a word to me, it was only to lob some oblique epigram, whose meaning was absolutely impossible for me to understand.

How I reproached myself for my impertinent timidity, what strong words I had for myself to make a better show of myself in the future: but I was fated to begin my career as a sot, and it was up to women even to cure me of so absurd an illness: they worked this cure with a success that I am obliged to give authentic testimony to; and the marchioness herself labored to heal me in her own way, so that if at the beginning of my subsequent affairs I had suffered setbacks in self-esteem, they were so minor & so soon repaired that they didn't touch my position nor affect my reputation in society.

I let the marchioness take several more baths before putting into execution my courageous resolutions: it was easy to see that her coldness for me increased with each passing day; I was finally afraid I would lose her altogether, & I drew more strength from that thought than from all the plans I had formulated until then: besides, ever occupied with my desire to supplant his Greatness, a tricky and tentative perspective for a proselyte who had a reputation to make for himself & who was still, at that time, quite far from the one he made for himself since then: I lay in ambush one day as usual, with less precaution however, when I saw the marchioness arriving at her accustomed hour; I don't know if she noticed me or not; it didn't seem impossible to me, but she showed no visible sign of it; I distanced myself to give her the freedom to pass; she was accompanied by a woman who carried the necessary linen for her; this third person disconcerted me, I don't know why I felt that her presence was too much: I walked a thousand times around the bathhouse without hitting on any special idea as to how to enter; I didn't even know finally when to stop, until I saw her chambermaid exit and take the walkway back to the chateau: we were at a considerable distance from each another. Let the reader judge for himself the satisfaction I felt for what I attributed to a chance occurrence: I made up my mind then and there, & I was only waiting for the moment when the chambermaid turned the corner and was out of sight – when I heard piercing screams coming from the bathhouse, & which I recognized distinctly to be the marchioness' voice: I ran like the devil & on opening the door, the first object I saw was the queen of my heart, practically naked, coming to throw herself into my arms with the outward signs of a most terrible fright.

Now, it is good to mention, to make this story more intelligible, that the bathhouse in question was situated on the bank of a large canal that cut through the park; a balustrade was erected inside this charming structure, with seats disposed tastefully and offering easy access to the water of this same canal: but getting back to my story, at that moment in time, for I am concerned lest a goodhearted reader should suffer a great deal of anxiety for the state I was in then, – all I could get out of the marchioness in these first moments of fright was that she had an aversion and a mortal terror of eels, on account of their resemblance to snakes, and that having noticed one in the canal, she shuddered for horror, unable to suppress the cries I had heard. I am aware of no antidote to counteract the bite of these strong beasts, much less the fear of them: but the first step I took had in some fashion dissipated the clouds that were obscuring my reason; I felt like myself again, ashamed of the amount of time I had lost, & quite ready to make up for it; I recognized what needed to be done to make everything disappear, at least for the moment, and with what ardor I went about the task! there was never a better opportunity to put into action the happy talents nature had endowed me with.

Imagine for yourself: a young man, nineteen years old, passionate, consumed by desire, holding in his arms a woman half-naked whom he idolized, in a solitary place, & believing himself amply rewarded: the most cold-hearted philosopher could not have resisted a similar scene, all the more reason for someone who prided himself on not being one, & what's more an abbot, a servant of the Church, a Doctor of the Sorbonne, a candidate to a bishopric, – to tell the truth, that was not even the half of it; I held in my arms my dear marchioness, reassuring her. "Be calm," I told her while planting hot kisses on her mouth; "be calm, all the snakes, all the insects, all the beasts of the *Apocalypse* cannot harm you, not now, not in the arms of a lover who adores you." (For the sacred has always been mixed up with the profane, & my amorous expressions still showed the effects of the profession's contagion.)

"Open your beautiful eyes," I continued, "& deign to confirm for me the indescribable happiness that chance has procured for me."

"Ah! my dear abbot," she said finally, with a sigh that I quickly gathered from her mouth. "How is this? you loved me, and you hid it from me? ah! you are cruel; let go of me, I don't ever wish to see you again."

Do you really think that I obeyed her? I'll let you decide. The virtue of the *little collar* was over-powering; I cannot recall it ever having had so much strength over me; it took away my ability to speak; the only thing I could do then was to kiss her and embrace her with a fury; I walked my ardent hands over her large, white, and perfectly buoyant breasts; I imprinted them with my devouring kisses; my soul, ready to soar, seemed desirous of joining itself with hers. My hands... happy hands! What didn't you touch! Nothing was refused to you! Gods, what intoxication! what voluptuousness! I was the master of everything; my dear mistress in a swoon and overwhelmed by sensual delight refused me nothing; all I heard anymore were some sighs and a few broken phrases:

"Let me be...," she said to me in a hushed voice, "I can't take it any more... I'm on fire... my dear child... ah! don't abuse the sweet love that I have for you...."

Too occupied to respond, I understood the value of the moment; everything was inviting me to consummate my happiness, vouching for my success. I saw, I touched, the charms worthy of the Gods themselves, for nothing blocked my view nor my tender caresses: the shape and line of her belly! how round! how white!... the shape of her thighs! what proportions! ... the small of her back! her hips the size of the Graces' themselves; her ass!... ah!....

I'm getting off track; it would be better to imitate that famous Greek painter who preferred to draw the curtains rather than paint things that are impossible to express: I can barely control the fire that the feeble image I retrace now inspires in me; & at the moment that I write this I feel that I am more abbot than ever.

I was amazing as the abbot then, in any case: so many adorable charms offered up to my amorous passion inspired in me desires that would have made me worthy of the Primate of the Gauls,[6] if that dignity alone could have been awarded me based on shining merit; I was no longer in control of the flame that consumed me & I gave up resisting the fire of my vocation. There was no comfortable place in this small room to communicate it to the marchioness; desperate not to lose so beautiful an instant of fervor, I was al-

---

[6]Primate of the Gauls: the French Archbishop, a Bishop who has precedence or primacy over the nation (in this case, of the Gauls, or France).

ready employing the baluster in a way that was, per-haps,[7] unknown to bishops and prelates; one under-stands my line of reasoning; I was about to give her a taste of its energy; &, in spite of the uncomfortable-ness of the position, I put forward the *DEFINITIVE ARGUMENT*: she was not without some distrust in its success, but I was going to destroy her disbelief. Al-ready we were united to the extent of being one, al-ready I was insinuating myself adroitly into her... heart; I had her half-way... persuaded, when the ac-cursed chambermaid whom we certainly were not ex-pecting, brusquely entered & surprised us; the mar-chioness was in a bit of a dubious position, & I was deploying my brilliant... state, covered in... glory; in such a state that, in a word, of all my honest readers and critics together, three quarters of them will be more envious of me than imitators.

The maid who was well-bred & not the least well-educated in this world, let out a small sigh of envy, bit her lip, turned her head, & rushed forward to help her mistress get dressed, as if she hadn't seen anything; as for me, I adjusted my clothing the best I possibly could & took leave of the marchioness, who thanked me without any embarrassment, & with a su-perior effrontery, for the service I had just rendered her, adding, with an expressive glance, that she would spare me my modesty by keeping this between our-selves, but that her gratitude was no less keen or real for all that. I understood perfectly her meaning; this last occasion was worth two Sorbonne theses for me,

---

[7]Original footnote: Note the "perhaps."

& it had enlightened me a great deal more.

She returned to the chateau a little while after I did, & two days passed before I received anything in particular from her; even though when her eyes turned towards me, they were always filled with love & sensuality: but I needed more from reality; the adventure in the bathhouse had only whet my appetite on a number of fronts, which I felt myself furiously prepared for; finally I was in such a state that I was unwilling to think of anything else, when Monseigneur received an invitation to attend the reception of a new abbess at an abbey where he had many connections; he didn't dare refuse, & the marchioness affected indisposition, which served to elude the offer he made to her to accompany him; a certain wink from her succeeded in enlightening me; I felt the master stroke, & I resolved, this one time, to act in a way that would guarantee my success in overcoming all supervening inconveniences. On the following day his Greatness departed after filling up on breakfast, which surely wasn't in imitation of the apostles; he was helped into his sedan, reminded to guard against drafts, not to overeat in the evening, to water down his wine, to avoid novices as well as young professed nuns, and finally to avoid a thousand tiresome situations and events that deprive us daily of our most distinguished prelates; & on returning to the house, the marchioness seized a favorable moment to set a *rendezvous* with me at the end of the day in his Greatness' rooms even, where we would have two hours of retreat, with the help of that eternal indisposition, that terrible shield, which everyone in the house respected, which nobody dared penetrate.

I showed up that evening at the assigned place, & I was let in through the door by the little maid in question, who, I might add in passing, had an extremely cute little face. I found the marchioness sitting back in a *duchesse,*[8] wearing the most sensuous negligee; her attitude was touching and voluptuous; one of her legs was extended entirely on the duchesse, & the other was off to the side with her foot resting on the parquet; her underskirt was almost entirely lifted by that split, allowing me see the knees of both her perfectly-shaped and proportional legs; her bosom, that adorable bosom that I adored, was nearly completely exposed to my view; her accelerated breathing made it rise & allowed me to see the whole of its beauty; her divine eyes were brimming with fire, with sensuality, which put me into an indescribable state: I approached her with joy; & taking up one of her hands, which I covered in passionate kisses, I could barely find the words to express to her what she inspired in me at that delicious instant. The marchioness was no less moved than me.

"It's you then," she said to me with a tone of voice that touched my heart, "I know how you are with your exactitude! I was beginning to be afraid that some coldness on your part..."

"Ah! how ever in the world could you think that," I responded to her, holding her tenderly in my arms, "& when all my thoughts, all my actions, are

---

[8]duchesse: a kind of reclining chair or *chaise longue* of sorts.

centered solely on you, – how could you accuse me of so cruel an injustice: if only you could read my heart! what transports! what love you would see there!"

"Ah, my dear abbot," she responded, "can I count on your oaths, & will I ever regret someday the confidences I place in you?"

She overcame me with caresses as she said this; she pressed my head to her bosom, which I clung to with my mouth; with joy, I went from one ivory-white, firm, admirably-shaped breast to the other; I got drunk on her, I was overcome, lost in love and sensual desires; however I was far from being perfectly satisfied, the occasion was too beautiful not to wish to advance it. What would my beautiful mistress herself have thought to find herself neglected, she who had sacrificed everything for me, who was leaving a prelate, an important and decisive man, and for whom? – a puny student.

I was perfectly aware how much I owed her in gratitude for so great a sacrifice, & I was quite prepared not to show myself ungrateful; in the agitation of our caresses, & our divers actions, my hands never remained idle; I had at first placed one, as if indifferently, on her knees, where that underskirt was located which I mentioned was working in my favor; I slid it up her thighs which were of a whiteness, of a shape... Finally I arrived at the theater of sensual pleasure, at the source of all delights; I hope you don't expect me to draw an exact picture of this; I am not at all, still today, free to describe just anything; besides, all the inexpressible joy that I felt led me more to the *reality* of pleasures than to a frivolous examination of them; those voluptuous touches put me in a state I could not resist; the marchioness was in a rather similar situation. How could I stop on so favorable an occasion, wouldn't I deserve to be cut off from that venerable body of prelates to which I belonged; I threw myself on her then with an inexpressible passion; she was laying back on the duchesse; I lifted her skirts, her breasts were bared: I kissed, I sucked, everything with a passion; at last, impetuously, I gave her the last signs of a love that had reached the breaking point.

"Ah!" she exclaimed, when she felt that our hearts and souls were melting together & after I had launched my frontal assault. "Ah! my friend... you persecute me... finish, I implore you... no... I adore you... ah! my dear abbot,... ah! I'm dying... Gods, what pleasure!..."

These broken phrases of hers were accompanied by several small movements that she made, feigning to want to free herself from my arms, & which only served to bring my sensual desire to a head; she looked at me with tenderness in her eyes: her eyes, faithful interpreters of the state of her soul, were blended with love, desires, & pleasure; a little fleck of foam like snow revealed itself at the edge of her charming lips, her breasts heaved and fell precipitously; at last we brought this delicious moment to a culmination by that burst of sensual delight that seizes & destroys all our senses, that brings shocks & shivers to the extremities of our bodies, when an image of divinity appears, or what one conceives to be a perfect pleasure, but which dies and disappears thereafter, and which, finally, is the work of a moment & whose passage is as fleeting as a thought that leaves us with merely a sad, cruel, & convincing testimony of our imperfection, & of the unhappy feebleness of our being.

Brought back to ourselves, & too caught up in our passions to entertain at a similar moment such distressing reflections, – how many charming things we said to one another! from then on, every constraint between us was banished, & I do not know anything so lovable, or so seductive, as the conversation that follows the first caresses of two young, impassioned lovers; that beautiful woman exposed all her tender feelings for me, & she had an inexhaustible fund of them; I responded with all the appearances of passion, which was enough to satisfy her for I see quite clearly now, by means of the trial I have gone through with regard to what excites true love in us, that what I was feeling then for the marchioness was merely a *need* to love (if that makes any sense), and that finally I was mistaken: at my age that was not surprising; it must not even appear extraordinary that she was mistaken as well; I had deceived her so well!

My desires and my youth aside, I had too great a respect for my profession to stop while I was ahead, & so as not to suffer a blow to a reputation acquired by the entire Body [of Abbots] & that I was beginning to share, my proofs were so reiterated & so sustained that I would have been equal to the severest test: the most passionate caresses, the most tender words succeeded one after the other with such rapidity that the hours passed like seconds; the night was already rather advanced when I left my voluptuous marchioness, & what occupied me the most at this moment was a desire to see her again: nobody had noticed, or they pretended not to notice, our absence, & in the company of our friends we armed ourselves with a seriousness and a gravity that alone could hide our mutual intelligence.

We profited by my uncle's absence, which lasted several days, to give proof of our feelings for each other at every instant; finally he returned, & we needed to take double precaution not to give him any reason for offense. I was unable in our various conversations to keep from remarking to the marchioness several suspicions I had about her liaisons with my dear uncle, but she had responded to me with such candor and ingenuity that, if she had not entirely dissuaded me, she had at least left me with a doubt that it would not have seemed proper of me to let her suspect, given the position we found ourselves in, & about which, I must confess, all the most curious investigations I was able to conduct since then were unable to procure any additional information that might have been to her disadvantage. He was, she said, her *FRIEND* for all time; & although I knew only too clearly just how much this word is abused between two young people & of different sexes, my having no proof that their liaison went beyond the limits of friendship, & receiving moreover everyday a thousand tokens of passion from the marchioness, I took the attitude of desensitizing myself to ignoble prejudices & of being content with enjoying the caresses of a charming female, without poisoning my happiness needlessly by an unfounded delicacy.

In spite of his Greatness' presence, we found a thousand moments during the day to give proof to each other of the liveliness of our love; all the most secret locations in the house & in the park were witnesses to our flame, & marked by the trophies of our love. It was all *DUCHESSES* and *SOFAS* for us; the most uncomfortable situations merely intensified the devouring fire that consumed us; my princess lent herself voluptuously to my transports; we were more enchanted with each other with each passing day. My uncle who was blind to us, as much as was needed to assure our happiness, added still more gas to the fire by the occasions he furnished us without realizing it.

One afternoon we were in his rooms with the marchioness, the rest of the company had gone out for a walk, when someone came in to inform his Greatness that the Agent of the Clergy was on his way from Paris to see him: he exited immediately, ordering me to stay put to keep that lady company, telling her that he had some serious business to attend to, which he wished to spare her the boredom of by receiving the Agent in another set of rooms; we submitted to that arrangement with an interior satisfaction that is easy to imagine; it was yet another tête-à-tête , & at our ages, in the heat of a new passion, one can easily figure for himself with what ardor we rushed to profit by this: persuaded that his visit with the Agent would be enormously lengthy, given that prelates never parted from each other's company without having first spoken ill of all their brethren in general, not to mention that on such occasions the nurslings of the Church have a very different charity than men of the world do; as soon as we were certain they were occupied, we lost no time imitating them, but in quite a different fashion: we were in the prelate's suite of rooms, & this simple fact, added to the pleasure of deceiving him & to the attraction that forbidden things naturally have, was the cherry on the cake for our sensual pleasures: after several kisses which always act as precursors on like occasions, & some petting which are necessary precursors, I took my charming mistress in my arms, & I threw her down on the episcopal couch. What softness! What luxury! What elasticity! We were nearly buried in the down that was going to serve as the theater of our amorous struggles. Let no one boast of worldly splendor to me, or of the conveniences that opulence communicates to the children of Pluto: lower the flag, modern Croesuses, lay down your arms, & humbly admit the difference between your superfluities and the holy luxuries that the Church showers on its servants: drab furnishings without pizazz, but with what taste! with what attention to detail! in what condition! Modest beds,[9] but what beds! What pillows! What eiderdown! Divine Providence, your decrees are as infallible as they are incomprehensible! But you, coward, were you among the blessed elect? what am I saying! You are still among them, & you are still able to form the culpable

---

[9]Original footnote: in terms of color.

plan of quitting the sacred flock so as to re-integrate with the perverse world, where the imperfection & insufficiency of the most vivid pleasures is a continual proof of the wide-spread malediction on all who do not inhabit the region of *PAPIMANIE*.[10]

We took a moment, the marchioness and I, to accustom ourselves to the beatitude that we were not at all made for: the hard bed of a billeted soldier or a Franciscan monk would have much better served our desires maybe; but in the end, what to do? we needed to mortify ourselves & take the bad with patience; the most intense caresses of mine cleared the fortunate route to pleasure; she grew agitated, & with each bound of sensuality Monseigneur's instrument of repose loudly creaked beneath us, unaccustomed as it was to so active and inconsiderate a treatment; my valor flagged only after some rough labors; I felt inside myself something extraordinary, which that predestined couch doubtless inspired in me; in the end, we got up after a long span of time spent in rapid continuous succession of the most intense sensual activity; & after having repaired, in the most adroit manner we possibly could, the small disorders that our amorous frolics had given to the arrangement of his Greatness' bed, we exited his rooms, after having spent one of the most voluptuous afternoons on record; we learned that Monsieur the Agent had hit the road again for Paris, & we were rejoined by my uncle who had gone on several walks around the gar-

------

[10]*Papimanie* (or Papimany): a fictitious land where the Pope and his court reside; from the third book of *Gargantua and Pantagruel*, by François Rabelais.

den before returning to the house.

He hadn't the least suspicion of the things we had occupied ourselves with during his absence, & we enjoyed again for some time the pleasures attached to a secret & well-executed intrigue. Finally it was time to return to Paris; my uncle, the marchioness, & all his company returned together, while I was obliged to follow them; not long after, I returned to the Sorbonne to complete my courses in theology & to make myself worthy thereby of the favors that were soon to be showered on me; meanwhile, I continued to see the marchioness assiduously, & although what I felt for her did not merit the title of true passion, I confess nevertheless that my liking for her was sustained with enough liveliness that our secret agreement could have lasted an eternity, when the Devil who is ever watchful, principally over the elect, got it into his head to trip me up in the most extraordinary fashion, to tempt my religion, & to hasten my rupture with the marchioness by a snare that any man would have fallen into, all the more so a man of my robe.

You will perhaps remember a maid I spoke of in the story of the marchioness' baths, & whose abbreviated portrait I had drawn: it was only in passing that I paid attention to her at that time; but finally, this same Time brings out everything, & rarely can one resist the events it gives rise to: I often found myself face to face with her; it was impossible that I would not notice her at last. Clairette, that was her name, had one of those fine and delicate, cute little faces that grow in beauty the closer one gets to them and studies them; she really had the prettiest shape to her face, the most mischievous eyes, the whitest and plumpest of breasts, the smallest foot, and, finally, altogether the freshest piece of ass you could ever have found, – and all this was, as if to say, offered up to me & at my disposal, for I was beginning to understand how to use simpering airs effectively, I was simpering already exceptionally well even; so I had caught this little wench several times looking at me with certain large languishing eyes that seemed to complain of the scant attention I was paying to their communication; I was listening attentively to what she wanted to say now, but how could I have wished or even been able to respond! Ever occupied as I was with the marchioness, how could I be distracted by another object? It's not that it wouldn't have been quite easy for me to nibble at her in passing; for I already had furious dispositions to reunite with the essential qualities of my state. I knew quite well that the proverb *lay it at the altar* had been made expressly for us; but either for stupidity, or for lack of opportunity, or for the ridiculous inseparable attachment to a first affair, I had pushed away from me all the little temptations of the profession that had presented themselves in this respect; I held firm to my one "love" as long as we were in the countryside; I resisted even a thousand, quite determined coquetries on the part of this little person: but it was in Paris at the Sorbonne where the devil lay in wait for me; a finer man than myself would have succumbed, as one will see.

I was holed up one day quite tranquilly in my room; I was studying, & I was reflecting on the most efficacious means to abridge a novitiate that was weighing on me strangely, when the College porter, whose palm I had greased for certain leniencies, came to let me know that at the door was a carriage with a young abbot in it, who was asking if I was visitable and alone, & who expressed much eagerness to see me; I had an infinity of acquaintances of my same age, so without stopping to guess who this might be, I simply told the porter to allow him in; he obeyed me, & a few moments later, after having heard a knock at the door, I advanced; what I thought I saw enter was a young ecclesiastic with a charming face whose features were unrecognizable to me at first; he drew near me while blushing.

"You don't recognize me," a touching voice said, unsure of itself. "Maybe, after all, that's in my favor; so hazardous a step as this could perhaps inspire in you a hateful contempt for the unfortunate Clairette."

Imagine my surprise. I stood confused and taken aback; the beautiful abbot, or Clairette, however she wished to be called, had fallen to my knees, & held my hands which she moistened with her tears. O love! or rather, o God of pleasure! How powerful is your appeal to an ardent, young heart; never have I been piqued with cruelty towards the finer sex, and besides, with that face – how could I rebuff so lovable a child, who came to place her fate, her life, and all her charms at my disposal; I helped her up off the floor, & I held her in my arms; I called her the tenderest names most suited to reassure her: meanwhile,

Monsieur the future Doctor of Philosophy was grow-
ing terribly hot under the collar; the enemy, who was
watching for my downfall, had surrounded and sur-
mounted me; I felt his redoubtable spur, which at every instant pricked my side with its fury; I knew no
better remedy for this temptation than to succumb to
it: shame on every reader and every critic who will
grant me no pardon: it is certainly a worse sign for
him than for me.

I smothered then with caresses my new bed-
fellow, & to spare her a confession that would have
redoubled her confusion I led her gradually toward an
alcove that concealed the lowliest of mean beds: I
didn't stop kissing her along the way & encouraging
her by everything I believed most suitable to overcome what little remained of a timidity natural to her
sex, especially after so bold a step; I had no sooner
made her sit on the bed when, unbuttoning precipitously her soutane, I placed my hands on her breasts,
whose blinding whiteness were infinitely more so by
the contrast of her dark clothing: Gods! What charms!
What beauties! I could not decide which of her two
breasts to prefer with my kisses and homage, so I
chose them both; I was drunk with sensual pleasure,
unable to sit down: Clairette, tender, half-vanquished
Clairette, no longer defended herself, not even feebly;
prey finally to the most intense transports, I succeeded in removing all her clothes and all the obstacles
getting in the way of my desires; happy abbot! what
charms fell victim to your hands & avid looks! Nothing at this point could have stopped me; all the Sorbonne could have tried in vain to make me let her go;

soon I pushed Clairette back on my bed, and I hastened her defeat and the enjoyment of my pleasures with a vigor that was quite necessary on that occasion; it was more like a massacre than the voluntary sacrifice of a victim: the blood flowed in great waves, the tears got mixed up in it, – precious tears! broken by burning sighs, followed by an inexpressible, sensual delight: M. the Doctor's mean bed groaned under the redoubled blows of the Sacrificer, but it was up to the test: a simple bed on like occasion is a priceless piece of furniture; if I had had Monseigneur my uncle's soft bed instead, we would have been lost, it would have busted, & we would have found ourselves lying on the floor buried beneath the debris of a thousand pieces.

Having survived our first drunkenness, my dear Clairette, emboldened now, confessed that she was in love with me at first sight, that she was defenseless against it, that her love had only increased during our stay in the country, that she had grown desperate by the indifferent attitude with which I had received all her marks of attention; that finally our separation having only intensified, instead of lessened, her longing, she had decided to use that disguise to come and offer up her heart and her body, & was resolved to take her own life if I had received her and her offering with contempt; I thanked her as best I could for the precious gift she had made to me, & imagining to myself that I would be in effect a craven villain if I took so few laps around such a beautiful field, I felt bound to begin showing her new marks of gratitude: our pleasures recommenced then with more lively vigor than ever; the modest bed again found its voice in the conversatio & was of marvelous utility to us: finally she left me after we had exchanged a thousand testimonies of most rapturous passion, & she promised me she would use, as frequently as she could, a disguise that kept our love a secret.

She kept her word, to the letter, & we enjoyed inexpressible pleasures together over the course of several months, while she visited me frequently; but I was too happy for that to continue: I had always kept myself in the marchioness' favors, & I had more than one reason for that, for she was the motivating force behind on my uncle's liberality, and she often supplemented it with her own, but it was not meant to be that I should cultivate two plants simultaneously without their becoming aware of my divided attention. Clairette well understood the necessity of sharing; besides, she was only mildly in pain, but the marchioness was not made of so easy a constitution: she immediately noticed the cooling of my attentions & the rarity of my homages, as I disposed of a fund that she had flattered herself to be all hers: too experienced to imagine that she could pry the truth from me & too dissimulating to make a *scene*, which would not at all have led to a clarification, she resorted to watching carefully my every step: soon, without my even knowing it, I was discovered at close hand, & she didn't take long to learn that a young abbot was paying me very long and very frequent visits; she learned with similar promptitude who it was & the betrayal that she suspected. To this day, I still don't know how she procured this information so quickly and so certainly, but however she did it her vengeance was as prompt as her information gathering; poor Clairette, the victim of her fury, was taken away abruptly and locked up in Sainte-Pélagie Prison, to serve as an example to handmaids who get it into their heads to please even better than their mistresses do.

For several days I was completely in the dark as to this catastrophe; but after not having seen her arrive as she was wont to do, on a day she herself had chosen to come and see me, nor the following day, I began to grow concerned: I was supposed to go and dine at my uncle's the following day; I set out before the usual hour, & I had myself presented at the marchioness' door; she refused to see me, which surprised me; I could not even obtain an explanation from the Swiss guard, & I was reduced to asking about, when some charitable neighbors instructed me that Clairette had been picked up without anyone knowing where she had been taken to, or why: I followed the road to the Bishop's mansion, distraught over this adventure, but quite far from anticipating what was waiting for me; my uncle received me with icy coldness:

"The king," he told me, "has just agreed to award you the Abbey of ***; it is a considerable benefice, & it is falling into ruin for your predecessor's fault; your meticulous and masterful eye will soon remedy this disorder no doubt, moreover it according to the rules that you should go and take possession yourself."

I turned pale upon hearing this terrible order; but imagine what became of me when I heard him telling me that I was to leave that very same evening, or enter the seminary on the following day: a mortal shiver ran through my veins; that terrible seminary frightened the hell out of me; on the other hand, to have to leave Paris, without knowing what had happened to Clairette, that poor Clairette who, because of me, had been done for: never in my life have I been reduced to so strange a perplexity; if that weren't already enough, the perfidious marchioness arrived on the scene, gay and triumphant; she congratulated me on my new promotion with a mocking and nasty tone, and pressed like a madwoman for my departure; so in spite of my ruses and vexation, it was settled: I had to leave that evening after supper; in vain did I try to escape under the pretext of needing to gather my old clothes at the college, but they had the diabolical charity of sparing me even this concern: they never lost sight of me for the remainder of the day, & at the moment of my departure, without entering into any detail, the Doctor of the Sorbonne, newly appointed Commendatory Abbot, was sent off in a sedan accompanied by an old ape, a chamber valet or governor, a species of amphibious animal with a surly face and humor who, to add insult to injury, was in control of my finances, to better rein me in, to the effect that I was forced to wait until my return to Paris to inquire into Clairette's situation. I rode to my Abbey in a fit of rage.

Part Two: Maturation and Rage

The memory of that unfortunate mistress occupied my mind throughout the course of my journey: it was not that I was taken by a violent liking for her, but I had always possessed a good and compassionate heart, & I was veritably touched by the fate of that poor child, whose downfall I had had a hand in in some way; but necessity obliged me to put a cap on my inquietude, until my return to Paris furnished me the occasion to be of more essential service to her than merely anguishing over her to no purpose: I also reflected long and hard over my place of exile, and on the life that I was destined to lead; I had a dreadful image of it in advance, given I had never been attracted to life in the country: I detested anything and everything that smacked of solitude: the woods, the natural fountains, the copses, the shade, the streams rolling their waves onto the argentine sands, in short all the treacly drivel that Messieurs the Lyrical Poets fill their insipid works with, all that, I say, had always filled me with an immense quantity of boredom, and not the least bit of desire. The place I was traveling to was far removed from big cities. I had, it is true, neighbors from Paris, titulars and people of good company, but it wasn't the season yet for them to live on their lands, & I felt in advance the amount of boredom I would have while waiting for them; that I would have to resolve on associating with country nobility, oh! there was no way: that would be equivalent to wishing to kill myself, to exposing myself to die for anguish and boredom; the only position then that remained for me to take was to be alone, & to construct castles in the air; for I had not one single book with me, & I was going to live with the most ignorant monks of all, who assuredly were more taken with wine cellars than libraries, & I could think of no topic of conversation we could have together that would lift me out of the boredom I was menaced with.

I arrived with these favorable prejudices, & I found nothing at first glance that was able to gainsay them; my future palace was an old Gothic building, rebuilt on several occasions, & made of a thousand scraps; the most dilapidated place was the church; even though we were still in a very harsh season, there was hardly one single pane of glass, which quite convinced me that it was not here that these gentlemen gathered most often: five or six large, dark figures, barded with scapularies, & fairly fat for country canons, came to receive me at my coach, and one of them regaled me with a compliment that he had happily forgotten three-quarters of, but who let me sample from the little that he did utter the rusty eloquence of country orators: I was led to my rooms through the abbey courtyard where I noticed, while passing, the inner courtyards filled with an impressive quantity of all sorts of poultry, which allowed me to obtain a fairly good opinion of my brothers' prudence; the inside of the house was more cheerful and comfortable than the outside seemed to promise; one always discovered, although of a much inferior kind to that of my uncle's, that modest care, that charitable attention to procure for oneself all life's comforts; my sleeping quarters moreover seemed to me the palace of sleep, the shape of the alcove and the furniture, the views even from my rooms, it all awakened in me a strong desire to spend two thirds of my life asleep, & the idleness invited me naturally to employ the remaining third of my time at eating and drinking: these were two points that my gentlemen brethren practiced religiously: in general, the interior of the house was rather well kept, but it was altogether something else when I saw the refectory and the cellar: What neatness! What cares taken to weatherproof & protect against the injuries of the seasons! It was easy to see that this was the most frequented location in the building: as for the cellar, it was immense, & although it was always the subject of lamentations by my brethren, I have seldom seen one that was so well-provisioned: it is true that it was often in need of reinforcements, but Providence had taken care to provide for it, & this was not a small testimony of its strength that it should be able to quench the thirst of so good a company: as for the church, I will not mention it again, it was the repair of all the rats & spiders of the surrounding area, who held a synod there that one scarcely interrupted. I will not however forget to mention here a particular trait of my brethrens' prudence, which was a chapel dedicated to I do not know what saint, but who infallibly healed everything: the canton had no reason to doubt it, & one saw attached to the wall a large number of arms, legs, & heads, whose bodies got along quite well because of this precaution, & nevertheless it was merely a matter of the inhabitants maintaining oil in some lamps & providing a habit to the saint on his feast day: to tell the truth, everyone needed to contribute, otherwise the saint caused the harvests to fail, the beasts to die, the women to give birth before their time, & a thousand other terrible disgraces and disasters that my humble brethren announced amicably, which warmed the faithful up, almost immediately, in terms of charitable giving, & ensured the presumed provisioning for the saint, but half of it was turned into wine & the rest into pieces of courtyard furniture.

My brethren, under the aegis of this small devotion, having secured an honest revenue and their being few in number, led a rather happy animal life: in addition, their amusements consisted in going hunting with the lesser nobility in the area, with whom they set themselves up as true children of the holy Church, that is to say that a legion of devils could not have dislodged them: they cajoled the women, got drunk with the husbands, went along with all their absurdities, got involved in their quarrels, listened patiently to their genealogy, played with them at checkers all day, & so on.

Judge for yourself, my dear marquis, whether such a life was for a man of my disposition, – whether it would not have been better for me to bury myself alive than to frequent such a company of people, – for that is also what I decided, & to lessen in some sort the boredom that threatened me, I asked, while trembling, to be shown to the library; one of my monks who was decorated with the imposing title of canon librarian got all worked up into a sweat to find the key; there was an embarrassment & terrible confusion in my flock at this news, the most ancient among them didn't remember ever having visited it; finally we were obliged to break the door down, M. the Librarian introduced me pompously into a large room decorated with four murals, where I noticed several books piled up in a corner & covered with dust; I immediately reviewed them; an army of rats scurried away at my first attempt to touch them: they consisted of several deteriorated and Gothic missals, an old edition of *François The Cook*,[11] a treatise on indigestion by a Cluny monk, & the *Eulogy of Drunkenness*, which appeared to be by the same author, who in an excess of modesty left it anonymous; I left these useful monuments where I found them, completely cured for the rest of my life of the curiosity to see another canon library.

My only resource consequently was solitude and daydreaming, until it should please my uncle to recall me to the terrestrial paradise that he had chased me out of: I imagined myself quite safely sheltered from any gallant adventures in so remote a location, when fate, which was preparing new adventures for me, created one that served to prove to me beyond a shadow of a doubt that control over the events of our life is something against which all the rules of human prudence will forever founder.

---

[11]*François The Cook*: *Le Cuisinier François*, written by François Pierre de La Varenne, published in 1651.

I had been living calmly in the abbey for several months when I was obliged to participate in some discussions regarding my prebends, & to go to B***, the episcopal village that I reported to; I spent several days there before my business was concluded, & having seen nothing among the two sexes that appeared to me worthy of either liaison or attention, I hit the road again as promptly as I could, back to my place of refuge. I was only about three leagues down the road, & about to leave the main highway in order to take a crossroad that led to my abbey, when my ears were accosted by some piercing cries a hundred paces away; I ordered my coachman to turn off in that direction, in spite of all ecclesiastical prudence that seemed to forbid it. I saw before me a carriage with six horses and a broken rear axle, which had turned over in the mud: I descended in a jiffy from my seat, & seeing a livery that was not unknown to me, I asked one of the men who his mistress was: he informed me that she was the Wife of the President de S*** who was on her way to her very beautiful country estate, two leagues away, & five leagues from my abbey; that she was in her carriage with her intendant and two of her women, & that she had lost consciousness because of the fright she had received: in effect, it was her women who had called out for help by loud cries; by my efforts & those of my men who accompanied me we succeeded in disengaging the carriage from the mud. Madame President had barely regained her senses when I recognized her immediately; I remembered having met her in Paris: she was young & had a charming face; I devised instantly the plan of starting up a relationship with her, & the reputation that I knew she had as a gallant woman was yet another reason to bolster me in my designs, & to make me hope for a happy outcome: she appeared to receive my efforts with gratitude, & regarded me even with some attention; according to my plans, I represented to her that her carriage could be of no more service to her until a cart wright from the nearest village had been sent for, which village was about one league away; I added that night was about to fall, it was not suitable for her to remain exposed to a thousand bothersome inconveniences on the main highway, & I offered to escort her back to her estate in my carriage, leaving her people with her own until it was ready for travel again: she made some signs of protestation, which I saw through and realized that she would not be upset to be pressured, so I insisted, & finally she accepted, with an appearance of confusion; I offered her my hand, she took it, & after having given orders to her people, we climbed into my carriage & hit the road in the direction of her landed estate.

We were no sooner alone when, knowing too well her reputation of being a gossip, I told her a story that, although old and tired, appeared to me still of good enough merit for that occasion: I made a real drama of it, I played surprised, worn-out, confused; I grew sad by degrees & soon I became frightfully melancholic; I wept even, for that is a gift I possess: I had tears at my command, & this is an essential point, & perhaps one of the most adroit baits to reel women in by; she asked questions about my condition, she began to grow interested; I sighed with the air of a hypocrite, I didn't respond, but it was all I could do to not burst out laughing: finally she appeared to soften to me, & she absolutely had to know the reason for so sudden a disappointment; I told her finally, with a Tartuffian tone of voice, that I attributed the hopeless adventure that had befallen me to none other than my unlucky star, without holding it in any way responsible; she asked me to explain, & when I put into play all the *lazzi* needed on such an occasion, I confessed to her with a trembling and studied confusion that I adored her for a long time, that I had had the opportunity to see her several times in Paris, without ever being able to find the occasion that would allow me to introduce myself, though I waited for it passionately; I let out a thousand moans about my fate that had caused me run into her again only to redouble my suffering & to bury deeper into my heart the arrow that was shredding me apart: finally, I acted the passionate & bashful lover, the novel's hero: fortunately what I had on my hands was a priss who, although she was ever ready to surrender, wanted to be approached according to form, & dominated by a sentiment that she never stopped playing; it didn't take long before I had turned her little head around in a way that it was a pity. She responded to me at first with all the commonplaces that facile sots employ in like cases: "Lovers are never satisfied... I remember your face now, and your cast of mind... I feel I would love you a lot, but you men are insatiable,... if I followed a penchant, you would soon start demanding things...."

I assured her quite positively that I had too much respect for her to act like that; I saw that she doubted what I was saying; I added protestations and oaths, & to get a better foot in the door, I began to pass the time planting kisses on her mouth & visiting her bosom just a bit.

"Stop right there," she said to me in a nonchalant tone of voice. "Ah! My little abbot, what a libertine you are! When I get back to Paris, I will tell your uncle."

I didn't respond to these threats, except by continuing my philosophical occupations: at this moment, we passed a place in the road that was quite broken up & where, by consequence, the shocks to the carriage were much more easily felt; she had fear of the carriage rolling over again, & she leaned entirely against me with feigned fright; I did my best to reassure her, knowing that in the field of the human heart the stronger feeling destroys the weaker one; I knew that there was one feeling stronger than fear, and I hurried to employ it. I took possession of her breasts with an imperiousness that she didn't dare dispute; one hand was busy at this office, while the other was free: I made it take a different route, a certain pocket presented itself, ideally suited to my purpose, & it led me directly to the sanctuary of pleasures by the secret stairway. She resisted again, but so feebly! She so desired to be conquered! Anywhere else this would have been the moment for me to triumph, & the field would have been taken immediately: but I feared the indiscretion of movements by the carriage, & the judgments that would have been made by my people who were riding behind the carriage; I contented myself then with certifying my rights, by re-connoitering the area & everywhere around it, and I succeeded in establishing them by the certain expedient that one employs on occasions when one can't do any better.

"Ah, let us put a cap on it, monsieur," she said to me, "but... what is this craziness here? Yes... in truth... this is quite spiritual... as for me I do not think... ah... ah... my good friend... my dear abbot, I'm hot... I cannot take it anymore... ah, finish up then... do as you please with me, then, alright?"

With these words & other suchlike trifles, we arrived at her estate where, while still holding a grudge, she invited me to spend several days with her: I was given the rooms of Monsieur the President who wasn't supposed to arrive until the holidays, & if I did not enter into possession of all his rights that very night, it was because it was not possible for us in the first commotion of making certain arrangements. I brought it up, however, and my proposal was received like a joke; but when I insisted strongly that it happen that very same night, I was told that I was out of my mind, & that I was to visit her in the morning after she got up, because she wanted to finish chewing me out then; I promised her this and kept my word, fully resolved to have her chew me out royally.

The very next morning, Madame President was in bed wearing a negligee that she had selected by design; I found her a thousand times more charming than the night before. In effect, she's a large woman with a good-looking body and a nice attitude, brown hair, with big dark eyes that speak volumes and say it in a terribly tender way! With an admirable waist, beautiful legs, small breasts, and very docile, as is fitting for women at a certain level of society, but all in all she had the bearing of a queen; she did everything in her power to chew me out, & I did my best to interrupt her: in the end, after several preludes, which I knew too well the price of to try to get out of, I threw myself at her, & covering her with kisses and caresses, I obtained her last favors as if by scaling the castle wall, & I plunged into a sea of delights that I had for so long a time been deprived of.

Madame President did everything that a woman of high society never fails to do in a similar situation; she sulked, she sobbed, she said she was quite miserable, that men were quite dangerous, that she never wanted to see me again, that she would never forgive me; finally she quieted down all on her own, for I was spiteful enough not to add anything of my own; & when I saw her calmed down again, I let her have it with enough advances to obtain more insults, which was the price I paid for having insulted her. One must understand that this lasted for only a short while; I satisfied her like a gallant knight, & our commerce was, from that moment forward, established with a confidence not seen in romantic novels.

I enjoyed for some time all the charms that are associated with a free and unencumbered, passionate love affair: Madame President was a unique woman for this type of affair; I was even figuring that with a similar pastime I could forget Paris, when I saw a certain big grey monk arrive, who was something of an entertainer and a dandy, an acquaintance from Paris whom she had enlisted to come and celebrate mass at the chateau, during vacation, & who was destined for more than one purpose, as I learned soon enough. The Observantist was a big, funny, brown-haired man with black eyelashes, squared and trimmed to his advantage, an alert eye, a beautiful and nervous leg, finally one of the most vigorous stallions in the Franciscan fold: he had a plump hand, meddled with music, scraped a tune on the violin, knew a thousand songs, a thousand quodlibets, a thousand country rebuses, making little remarks on the sly to all the maids and setting his sights on the mistress, having his way with all the women within one hundred yards, until finally here he was. Madame President, who was in on it, retained him; I don't know if he was one of my predecessors, but it didn't take me long at least to be convinced that he was chosen as my successor.

I had won over to my side, by my caresses & by my presence, one of Madame President's handmaidens, who furnished me the means to shed light on what I suspected; one afternoon I pretended to go back to my abbey, but I returned without being seen, and I had myself introduced into a closet that adjoined Madame President's bedroom; a glass door covered by a curtain hid me from view, & the first object that struck me was my dignified mistress in an exceptionally thin outfit, suitable for her business at hand, with the robust monk who approached her all resplendent with glory & performing things capable of overwhelming and revolting a person even, by how scarcely and rarely such things are seen. I confess that whereas I expected something of the sort, I was speechless at the sight of it; but my astonishment and my rage didn't take long to come to the tipping point when I saw Madame President go along with the Franciscan's transports of lubricity, who, after some quick warm-ups and feeling perfectly aligned in his needs and the dictates of his robe, threw her down on a couch where, after taking off his inconvenient jacket, he took tyrannical possession of all the charms I thought were my domain & started on a joust that was as rude as it was disagreeable for a spectator as interested as I was to observe. I was suffocating with rage in my hiding place, – twenty times I was on verge of exiting & subjecting these two miserable creatures to my wrath, but the fear I had that my vengeance would not be complete enough & that, seeing themselves without any witnesses, they would have the effrontery of denying everything, held me back in spite of myself & made me postpone what I was quite resolved not to let go unpunished. There was no longer any question in my mind about the consummation of the sacrifice: the Cordelier[12] was not the sort of man to leave me the least consolation on that score. If I had been incredulous, for I would have wanted to deny my eyes & not lend any credence to his first proofs, but he was about to provide successively a rather large round of additional proofs to vanquish the thickest incredulities I had; I considered myself warned; I

---

[12]Cordelier: a member of the Franciscan order of Observantists. By the name "Cordelier" one also understands better perhaps the "cord" of St. Francis used by Father Dirrag in *Theresa the Philosopher* (Sunny Lou Publishing).

understood people too well to retain the least hope, besides I was suffocating with rage seeing myself so cruelly played, & I left them to go meditate more calmly on the resounding vengeance I was resolved to inflict on them.

I had with me two of my men in whom I had enough confidence, & whom I had taken up with after the death of the old buzzard who had accompanied me from Paris; he had bothered to pass over to a better life, in which he had done me a signal service: I had him replaced by two amusing fellows I was sure of, fearless and unscrupulous men, with an honest dose of libertinage; in a word, just what a young man needed; one of the two had gained the good graces of the handmaid who would be useful to me, which favored our project even more; I didn't hesitate to learn through this conduit that the monk spent every night with Madame President, during which she could delude herself into thinking she would never be interrupted; I formulated my plan based on this information: several days later, I feigned a trip to my abbey, which happened almost every week: I took leave of Madame President, & I returned at twilight through a gate to the grounds that the maid had gone out of her way to open for us; we hid ourselves, me and my men, in a small farmhouse that was connected to the chateau; towards the middle of the night our confidante came out to alert us that his Reverence was between two sheets with Madame President, & she quietly let us into the house.

When I heard this news, I experienced an

emotion mixed with joy, rage, & vexation; I was also overcome by the certainty of what I feared, as if I should not have reasonably expected it. Perfidious women of the female sex! I said to myself, how can I trust you anymore when I see a woman, who only a few days earlier lavished on me the most passionate caresses, suddenly drop me, & for whom? For a monk, that is, for the dregs, for nature's opprobrium; I could not stop marveling at how a woman, well-born & cultivated, had let her bones be jumped by that contemptible type; I will not try to describe the emotions I felt, perhaps vanity entered three quarters into it; whatever the case, I was neither old enough, nor in the right place, to examine the nature of my feelings; I gathered all that remained of my sangfroid to post my men, as we had agreed, as close as possible to Madame President's rooms. Everything seemed to conspire to the success of my plan: Madame President's domestics, who were small in number, cowardly, and effeminate, were sleeping in a wing separated from the main body of the building where we were; the maid, according to plan, had me posted near her mistress' bedroom, & I began to shout "Robber!" at the top of my lungs; the noise penetrated as far as the bed, & I heard through the door the first signs of their fright; concerned lest the beggar should escape my vengeance, I promptly entered into the room where they were lying together in bed, followed by my two determined lackeys, each of them armed, like me, for any event, with a pair of pistols & moreover a whip, a terrible instrument and very necessary for the play's denouement. I turned a lantern that I held in my hand on high when I reached the bed. Imagine the amorous couple's surprise to see so unexpected an apparition; I was like a second head of Medusa for them: they were petrified; to the several discourses that escaped Madame President's mouth in the first commotion of her anger and shame, I didn't respond but two or three laconic phrases, which instructed her in so many words as to all the contempt she inspired in me. As for Monsieur the monk, he didn't get off so easily; he jumped precipitously out of bed & looked for his clothes & an escape route; my men permitted him neither the one nor the other; on my signal, they let their vengeful, pitiless whips fall on his back: the poor devil screamed and howled, which filled me with infinite joy; he was quite a ways away from the brilliant state he had been in when I was a witness to his prowess through the glass door, – exceedingly humble and in a crouching position: what was particularly enjoyable was Madame President's attitude during this scene; my sniggering really got her goat in a strange way, and she vomited on me a thousand invectives, which succeeded in filling me with great joy. My men who had my orders, after having regaled the Franciscan like a naughty boy from a good family, gave him intentionally an opportunity to escape: he didn't fail to seize at it & escape while hurling dreadful howls throughout the rooms, so as to gain the court, & to find some shelter from our rage; but that was precisely what we were anticipating, and we pursued him, chasing him like a hare, & continuing to flick the dust off his shoulders: finally, ever in pursuit of him, we arrived at the large courtyard of the chateau, where we found several half-naked domestics who had run there to understand the reason for so terrible a racket; the sight of a pistol, which each of us carried in our hand, impressed them enough to let us achieve our vengeance; Madame President cried at the top of her lungs from a window that someone should apprehend us, that we were wretches, robbers, assassins: several words from us sufficed to stop that rabble in their tracks & to inform them of the story in a few words; they stood there overcome and speechless: however, we didn't stop picking on the poor devil, the blood was flowing from both sides of him: at last, seeing that he had no means to escape our rage, he got the bright idea, despite the rigor of the season, to throw himself headlong into a trough of water designed for horses and livestock. Satisfied by my vengeance, & content with leaving him in a place so capable of cooling the fires of his lubricity, we exited without anyone daring to make a move or try to stop us, & I rejoined my carriage at a remote location where it was waiting for me; I found there the maid who had so well served us, who had judged it inappropriate to run the risks of remaining with her mistress after having rendered her a suchlike service: one of my men had promised to marry her, so I took her in without a second thought, & we hit the road that led back to my abbey.

On arrival, I found letters there informing me that my father was near the end of his life, and that he wanted to see me; I was advised not to defer my departure one moment: this news afflicted me a great deal, but on the other hand I felt some satisfaction leaving an area where I imagined the scene from earlier would not fail to be incessantly divulged; besides, having no other kind of amusement that could make me wish to stay, I bid my canons *adieu*, which I hoped would be forever, & without further delay I took the road for Paris.

En route, I could not help reflecting somewhat on the adventure that I had just gone through; there was no doubt in my mind that it would redound to Madame President's dishonor in a big way, & that by necessary consequence my name would get mixed up in it, disagreeably for a man of my robe: I realized the unpleasant repercussions and harm it would have on my uncle's plans for me, & I made a firm promise to myself from then on to be more circumspect about the women I got involved with; for doing completely without them didn't figure at all into my plans: consequently, then, I planned to avoid similar scenes from happening in the future; but I was not quite there yet, as one will see. On my return to Paris I found that my father had just passed away, & that my brother was caught up in the ordinary difficulties that always resulted from successions: I had seen very little of him until then; the occasion to speak about him during the course of my story had not naturally presented itself until now. You knew him, dear marquis, and you know that I am not at all exaggerating when I say that because of the advantages of his person as well as those of his mind and character, few knights in France could compare with him; add to this a gentleness and cordiality that he had with respect to me, I soon forgot the injustice that fate had played on me in the unequal division of goods: we loved each other dearly, & in all affairs that involved him regarding my father's succession, no decision was made that I was not consulted on. On his departure from the Musketeers, with whom he had participated in two campaigns, the Court had conferred on him the assignment of a company of cavalry in the regiment of ***. With spring approaching, he was obliged to leave Paris immediately and join his corps who were going to assist the Flemish army; he gave me a general power to finish all his affairs, & he remained confident in my friendship that I would see to concluding them in the most advantageous manner possible.

In the middle of all the cumbersome details that my current position, regarding our family affairs, had thrown at me by necessity, the occasion arose naturally to receive a visit by the marchioness, & as I had the appearance now of an important and determined individual, I approached her with an audacity that spared me at least three quarters of the sulkiness she was preparing for me; I even believe that it would not have been impossible for me to strike up my relationship with her again, if the news of my recent adventure with Madame President, which was all over Paris by the time I arrived, hadn't earned for me a reputation capable of chilling the most intrepid of women; the marchioness was too prudent a person to expose herself to a vengeance that she could not help meriting; so from this moment forward we acted as allies; all that I could get out of her was to learn the news of Clairette, whom she informed me had left Sainte-Pélagie & married an honest bourgeois man,

who made her extremely happy; I learned with infinite satisfaction that this poor girl's misfortunes had
come to an end, & perhaps I would have sought to
rekindle my relationship with her if I hadn't found
myself by chance in an unexpected adventure & had
precipitated myself again into the kind of life that I
had so resolved to avoid.

Among the hereditary matters I was in charge
of, I found the papers of an important lawsuit my
family had against M. the Duke de *** regarding land
boundaries; we were neighbors, that's sometimes
enough to become irreconcilable enemies, & while
the basis of the case was not important in itself, vanity played the greatest part in it, & it was otherwise
very susceptible to accommodation. In the time that I
spent fervidly, and with astonishment, pouring over
the immense grimoires[13] that this dispute had occasioned, I was paid a visit by an old lawyer whom I
knew by reputation to be a very enlightened and gen-
tlemanly sort of man; I had him seen in, & I was not a
little surprised when after the first polite remarks we
had exchanged he informed me that he was for a long
time now in charge of the affairs of the house of ***;
& that M. and Mme. la Duchesse de ***, having
heard about the death of my father & that my brother
on his departure had left me in charge of all our family affairs, had ordered him to come and confer with
me to bring an ancient quarrel to an end, which quarrel my father's inflexible character had dragged out

---

[13]grimoire: literally a book of magic or sorcery. But here the
meaning is clearly that of a text of obscure meaning (as legal
documents often are).

indefinitely; & they hoped that I would show myself to be more accommodating: he added to this discourse all the courtesies that could flatter me even more. I had heard mention of this affair & even of the members of my family finding fault with my father's obstinacy on the subject. As soon as we got into some details & I recognized how reasonable and moderate his propositions were, I had no objection at all about moving forward with the matter, assuring him that it would not be because of me if all was not concluded to the satisfaction of those who had sent him, & he left very surprised by what he called the unprecedented moderation in a young man, not to mention very satisfied by my reception of him.

As I have never had because of my birth certain country prejudices that make one get all tied up in knots over a first visit to someone, I didn't consider it a low or hazardous measure to go directly to the mansion of ***. I was announced and introduced immediately into the duke's rooms, who on my name alone came before me & heaped on me courtesies and tokens of friendship: he added that he was embarrassed that, not having expected me, he was up to his ears in some personal affairs that he needed to attend to; but he told me, while bantering, that "I leave tomorrow to join my regiment; consequently, it is not with me you will have to deal; I am going," he continued, while taking me by the hand, "to lead you to your adversary; defend yourself as best you can because I warn you, – you will have a tough opponent in my wife."

And with that, he led me into the rooms of the duchess, who was still in bed, & who was quite unprepared for such a visit: she concealed her surprise, & received us with all the simpering airs appropriate to a woman of her rank.

"This person here, madame," said the duke on entering the room, "is M. the Abbot de T***, whom I bring before you; you know that I am leaving, & that I cannot discuss with him the business matters we have in common; I leave this matter in your hands; I warned him as a friend that you were sharp as a tack, that he should be on his guard with you; I will leave you now; it is up to you to make the best deal that you can." And with that, he exited the room, with a light and detached attitude, & beseeching me to stay put; he left me in a tête-à-tête that I was far from anticipating the outcome of.

Until he left, I had paid little attention to the duchess' charms, barely even laying my eyes on her; but from the moment we were left alone, I felt that this affectation could no longer serve as an excuse, given the necessity I had to continue the conversation with her.

"Hey there, M. the Abbot," she said to me, in a lively tone of voice; "it sounds like we are to have some big discussions together, & may I expect to see them come to an end soon? I confess that I am charmed to learn that all this has fallen on your shoulders: I have heard all the world singing your praises, & I flatter myself that in no time I will have reason to join in with the *vox populi*."

I got a good look at her on the sly as she spoke. Although she was not a regular beauty, I confess I had never in all my life seen a more seductive body; her nightgown had something amorous and tender about it that completely tore me up in side: a range of ribbons negligently tied gave me a glimpse of a divine pair of breasts, adroitly attended to, & which nothing could equal in whiteness; a prodigious quantity of the most beautifully blond hair in the world fell in curls over her breasts & set them off even more brilliantly. She had shapely hands and arms, & her divers movements permitted me to consider them at my leisure; in the end, I saw nothing that wasn't the fountainhead of a thousand delights for me: all these little observations occupied me to the point that I remained for several moments without responding to her; finally, after pulling myself together little by little, I responded in terms that could best persuade her of my disinterestedness & of my deference to her wishes; I believe even that I let escape some words and phrases that must have made her suspect something of the impression she made on me; she was too much the high-society woman, & she possessed too much experience, to have been mistaken about it; & the tender eyes she soon darted at me gave me immediately a ray of hope; however my visit lasted an enormous amount of time without my realizing it. Finally she rang for one of her handmaids & asked for permission to get dressed; suddenly I realized my error & rose with a disconcerted air to take leave of her.

"Oh, for that, – what madness!" she said to

me, in the most engaging tone of voice; "where will you go at this hour? It's late: you will dine with me; I am alone; don't you want to keep me company?"

"But, madame," I said to her, stammering some poorly expressed thanks, "you infinitely honor me... I could not hope... I would be mortified to abuse your politeness...."

"That's very charming of you," she said, looking at me with tender affection. "I'm enchanted: but look, Abbot, it's fine for the first time: in the future you have to do away with all the compliments, – they exasperate me. I tell you once and for all, don't stand on ceremony, and *that's that*."

On saying this, she got out of bed, taking some precautions simply for form's sake, but so slightly.... One of her maids had entered, who helped her to put on a dress. What a lovely disorder... what a charming nature... what didn't I see at that happy moment! I will swear to you, dear marquis, M. the Doctor of the Sorbonne was in a terrible agitation; I had a dreamy and embarrassed look about me; I could barely make out the objects around me, & I hadn't even noticed that the maid had left & that we were left alone again.

"The poor fellow," said the duchess, approaching me. "He dreams, he is consternated, there is a *rendezvous* I am making him late for, oh that is clear! Confess it then," she said, "it's an affair of the heart that distracts you; to be honest, I'm a good person, all things considered; I will know how to put an end to your captivity: I will even be your confidante if you like; I'm an excellent person for advice, & the most tender passions touch me to an unimaginable degree."

There I was, a young man dominated by his passions, in a position to satisfy them, never denying them anything, – an abbot in a word, resisting such determined coquetries made above all by a young and charming woman for whom everything finally says only too much: I make my appeal to you, illustrious colleagues; justify me while reading me, take my side against cold old age & the vile Cagots;[14] tell me what you would have done in my place. I can imagine what you will decide, – it is that of Rousseau's Cordelier: eh, well, you see in me a worthy Candidate: *she was it, or the plague take me.*

The duchess, expressing herself as I have just said, playing with my hair with the one hand, readjusting her breasts with the other in such a way that, far from my losing sight of anything in that arrangement, I discovered a thousand more charms that are beyond words: these objects had brought my feelings to the point that I was unable to contain myself: I was on fire, I was consumed with desire, I fixed my enflamed eyes on her.

"What are you looking at? Lower your eyes," she told me, while placing her hand over them. "I don't know, but it seems to me that they are telling

---

[14]Cagots: a minority people in the southwestern part of France who were treated like the pariah from about AD 1000 to the 19th century, for unclear reasons.

me a thousand things I do not hear at all."

"Ah! Madame," I exclaimed, transported by my love or by my desires, by whatever one wants to call it in the end. "Ah! they only feebly give the impression that you have made on me, – would that you could read in them all that you inspire in me! I feel I'm losing my way here by speaking with you so freely, but I cannot help the powerful love I feel for you; a single moment has made my defeat; the same moment doubtless will be the cause of all my misfortune." (Confess it, my dear marquis, that I have captured the vapidity of our ancient Romans rather well here.)

"But, not at all," retorted the duchess, "what an idea! I'm not at all offended by such things; if a woman got upset by every declaration, she would need to bury herself in the desert & renounce living among humankind altogether. It's an accepted usage: one says that one loves, one swears by it, it becomes what you make of it: a woman is exposed to such things on a daily basis, but a woman is quite simple if she prides herself on it...."

I interrupted her to employ all the oaths, all the protestations, all our gallant hero's commonplaces, which I had a great store of, ready-made.

"Ah," she said, "no oaths please, – they bore me to tears, they infuriate me: certainly you don't expect to take me by surprise, do you? – that would be an extravagant idea: come on," she said to me, while taking me by the hand, "let's go eat; I need a breather, time to reflect, & to make my plans: what do I know? Perhaps after all I will be foolish enough to believe you, & you will gain more than you will lose."

We had something to eat, & I saw her arm herself with a different physiognomy than what I had just seen, & which had so pleased me; the conversation during the meal was of indifferent matters: truth be told, our eyes did their thing, but it was in a language that was all their own, & which was indecipherable by the people we had to guard ourselves from. After the meal, we returned to her room, & I saw for the second time the animated visage of that voluptuous enchantress, which alone made my joy; the conversation picked up where it had left off: she felt a natural liking for me; my face, my eyes, my way of saying things all pleased her: but no standing on formalities, no considerations to pay attention to! No fear of abruptness, nor indiscretions, nor, in a word, a thousand faults attached to my youth! I felt, however, that if one were to be allowed a single weakness & to succumb to it once in a lifetime, it should be with someone who really deserved it: judge for yourself the effect that like discourses should have on a man who had always prided himself on not being ungrateful; I was no longer in control at this moment of moderating the transports of my gratitude.

"No, beautiful duchess," I picked up the conversation again, holding her in my arms ardorously. "No, you will not at all regret what a happy penchant makes you do in my favor."

Happy Abbot! How will you ever be able to merit or pay for so precious a gift! While speaking like this, I had taken her in my arms, fully resolved not to deny myself of it by sterile discourses & cold protestations; I covered her with burning kisses on the mouth, which she offered to me, intelligent woman that she was & who knows her world; next, her bosom became my prey: a pin that had just popped out had uncovered it, leaving it completely bare to my avid glances and hands: all this scene took place while standing up in front of a fireplace; I felt the quarter of an hour to be decisive: the duchess didn't resist me any longer, I heard only some broken sighs, certain presages to an impending rout: I feared lest reflection should drag the comedy out too long; I was pressed to bring it to its denouement; I carried her quickly to a couch, & I threw myself on her.

I had barely taken possession of a place when I prepared to put the finishing touches on my happiness.

"But," she cried out, "goodness gracious!... what you are doing now is an extravagance!... think on it! What do these actions mean?... Is this how you treat a woman like me? In all honesty, I'll need to stop seeing you... ah stop this then... you are an imprudent... oh, effectively!... that's well done... my women could come in again... besides, I haven't locked the door... my Swiss guard is drunk... he will let all the universe in...."

During all this respectable monologue, I didn't lose a beat, & I was quite resolved not to drop a stitch: I took possession of her in a way as not to be stopped even if she did resist: I held her turned over beneath me, & I had succeed during this time in having almost completely undressed her: at last I came to the decisive conclusion of all that I was desiring.

"Ah, monsieur," she said to me, as soon as she felt my first attempt, "ah, stop please... you are killing me... you are suffocating me... ah, righteous heaven!... you are a monster... ah, that is detestable... effectively... I would have prepared myself... clearly you didn't count on my complacency... monsieur!... I say for the last time... you are hurting me, this is dreadful...."

I had "arrived" by this time, & I hadn't the good fortune to realize what was causing so many outbursts, when a cursed whistle blew which could be heard throughout the courtyard and which obliged me to stop dead in my tracks & pull myself together quickly; the duchess followed my example. What was amusing about this was that each of us was occupied in repairing as best we could the disorders of his appearance, without exchanging a single word: finally, a visitor was announced, & I withdrew, as is the custom, without taking my leave, when the duchess came running after me as far as the antechamber with a freedom of spirit that I couldn't help admiring.

"You are leaving, Monsieur Abbot," she said to me, "but why? I have a thousand things to speak with you about, & our lawsuit, – when will we finish up? Come sup with me the day after tomorrow...

wait... yes... the day after tomorrow... I will be free, & we can speak about this; I will go to the Opera, I'll be in a small loge; because I imagine that I will be dying of boredom, you will come and join me, and I will lead you back... you will come, yes? I am too good," she added, approaching my ear, and speaking softly: "I'm not at all obliged to forget your foolishness so easily, but in any case now I know how better to prepare for your needs."

I assured her, while looking at her straight in the eye, that I was hoping to better fulfill her next time, & that she would not find any reason for similar reproaches of me.

"Go away," she said to me, "you're a traitor, & I wish something terribly bad happens to you for all your mischievousness."

I took my leave of her, repeating to her the assurances of my exactitude, & quite resolved not to give her any future occasion to complain.

It was not difficult for me in the two days preceding our *rendezvous* to procure for myself some information on the duchess, which went a long way toward diminishing the opinion I had of myself, of my good fortune, & of the power of my charms: I was furnished with a long chronology of my titled predecessors, not to mention passing fancies and deceptions, & I was assured very positively that I would not be her last beau. But, after all, what did this clarification matter to me, – has a similar thing ever stopped a sensible man & prevented him from starting up an affair with a woman, whomsoever she might be, provided all his needs were met? The duchess was marvelous for what I wanted to do with her, & I did everything in my power not to let such agreeable future moments escape because of the stupidity of a miserable prejudice. I showed up at the exact moment I was expected, at the door to her loge at the Opera, as we had agreed: she cried for joy on seeing me.

"Ah! So there you are, you are charming to be so on time, I was waiting for you; the Opera annoys me to no end; but to the point: we will not sup at my place, we have to speak about serious things; I imagined that to be more at ease, it would be better to sup at my hideaway; it's delicious; I will be charmed if you can see it." At this same moment, she rose from her seat and offered me her hand, I escorted her to her carriage; we mounted it, after I had sent my carriage home, and we departed.

We arrived at her hideaway which was situated in the Fauxbourg St. ***. I realized that she had not exaggerated at all in what she had told me; it was charming, & I have seldom seen so voluptuous a place since then: all the rooms were tiny, but decorated competently & filled with charming furnishings in the most exacting taste, less sumptuous than comfortable: mirrors, admirable paintings, a garden maintained with extreme care, & not one view into the house or garden from without; we entered a room where everything invited sensual pleasure and lethargy; the weather was not at all beautiful enough to profit from the beauties of nature outside, but I could not tire of admiring those things within: I saw only sofas, duchesses, armchairs, chaise longues, and an infinite number of cushions: the most sensual paintings decorated the walls of this charming hideout: finally everything breathed of love & sensual pleasure in this dangerous place. These objects, which I was not at all yet accustomed to, filled all my senses with emotion, which was easy to detect.

"Hey," said the duchess, after we had settled in. "What do you think of my hideaway? don't you find it rather cozy? & doesn't it inspire in you the desire for a retreat?"

"Ah! Madame," I responded to her, looking at her with tenderness in my eyes; "what would be the point of my telling you all that this place inspires in me! You would condemn it doubtless, & the manner in which you received..."

"Ah! You are going to start up again with your foolishness," exclaimed the duchess. "Listen, I am in a terrible mood this evening, we will inevitably have a quarrel, and you will doubtless want things from me," she said, while trying to blush, & holding her hand in front of her face to prevent me from seeing that in spite of her efforts she was not turning red at all.

"As for me, madame," I continued, in the most tragic tone of voice I could possibly muster, "heaven help me from making an attempt on your virtue, which I have only too many cruel proofs of; I foresee the outrageous contempt with which you will ever reward the purest flame that ever existed; despair is the only recourse left to an unfortunate wretch...."

"But what kind of crazy talk is this?" interrupted the duchess, vexed, "if that isn't the most exaggerated and unprecedented capriciousness I have ever heard! Ah, monsieur, in all honesty, when a person is in a mood, he must keep it to himself, and not dump on others all the visions occupying his little brain: effectively, nothing is so *delicious* as this tiff I'm enduring: monsieur graces me by saying that he loves me, I dare to take the liberty of doubting it, he insists, & the next moment he is treating me like a woman *with poor marks*, like a woman pounding the pavement, a passing fancy, in a word a woman without mores & of bad company; he undertakes things, at first indecent and revolting, not to mention absurd, impossible, or at least unprecedented for me until now; & because one resists as any reasonable woman would do, because she does not jump straight into the sack with him, because she wants to take a moment to consider, to examine her thoughts, to make plans, in a word to proceed like a sensible human being, monsieur is rebuffed, desperate, ready to attack, to throw a tizzy fit, oh! For *that*.... But tell me then, abbot, honestly, you are a strange man, who have you been with then? Who do you actually know? What are your connections? What good families do you call on? Because in all good conscience, one cannot believe that you have spent much time in polite society."

I was laughing up my sleeve during all this excellent show.

"Do not ask me who I have been with, madame," I rejoined, pushing the villainy to the point of tears. "You make me forget everything, everything vanishes before you: this enchanting idea alone will be either my happiness or my unhappiness in life: it is not..." I continued in an earnest tone of voice, while drawing her near to me, and taking her in my arms as I felt myself worthy of the prize I had dared to aspire to; and I continued, planting hot kisses on her mouth and neck, "... I cannot deny myself the final satisfaction of telling you that you will miss me one day, – a tender and impassioned lover, who, alas, was mayhap worthy of you by the honesty of his feelings."

The comedy that we were acting in, the two of us, amused me too much to want to risk interrupting it too soon; I had resolved to leave to the duchess the satisfaction of pushing it to the extreme.

"Ah! What delights we would have enjoyed together," I exclaimed, while pushing her back in her bergère,[15] and taking the greatest liberties with her: "But no," I added, "your cruelty robs you of all those delights, leaving you only the sterile satisfaction of despairing of a lover who adores you." I didn't relinquish the prize while speaking like this; I had meanwhile pushed aside all the duchess' clothing that could still get in my way....

"Ah! Stop," she exclaimed, when she felt that I had gotten to the same point where I had left off the last time. "What behavior... you are an unusual man...

---

[15]bergère: an 18th century style upholstered armchair with an exposed wooden frame.

you scold people... you find them unjust... unreason-able... and then you want... ah! monsieur... is this any way to behave?... goodness gracious!... I will tell you again today... *that* will not happen... now look here... ah gods... he's a monster... this is unprecedented... without example... unbelievable... imagine for your-self that I cannot accept..." (note here that I was all the while going about my business) "but what an idea...you can see for yourself that that is not nego-tiable... ah!... that's better... I was going to tell you... you are very stubborn... ah, my God!! Monsieur... I am a dead woman... you are...."

She didn't say anymore. I pulled back as far as I could, in order to hear all her *lazzi*, which amused me to no end, but at last something final was in order, & I was obliged to resume my frontal assault, I suc-ceeded then without paying any attention to all the obstacles she wanted to honor me with. What can I say, I was born modest & by consequence an enemy to misplaced praise: in any case, I have to admit that I have undertaken few things in life more easily; but I will confess also that as soon as the playacting stopped & we found ourselves at the moment of ec-stasy, never have I known a woman who could better season it, by both a thousand terms & a thousand ten-der discourses that she addressed to me in the heat of passion, as well as with an endless number of bounds, movements, and charming caresses that intoxicated me with inexpressible sensual delight.

One knows rather well that after the first act I had nothing more regrettable to endure than to watch her have her fifteen minutes of shame and sulking, as all women like to do in like situations, but which was soon brought to an end & repaired by the thousand pleasantries that high-society wit and habits furnished her with and which she possessed in spades; I behaved myself that night, in a way that was designed to give her a strong positive impression of me, & I must admit that I enjoyed a thousand charms what with her embraces & her conversation; she had an air of honesty and passion about her, which would have impressed me if I hadn't been so precisely informed as to her character; she made out as if to adore me, to respect me even, which was admirable, given the motive:[16] finally we made arrangements to see each other every day; she never left me without the sad looks of the Heroine of the Opera: she made me promise a hundred times to see her again in the evening, for it was five o'clock in the morning, & I left her enchanted by her, not believing a single word she said about her passion, but quite satisfied by her charms, & very determined to make the most of them as humanly possible.

I kept my word to the letter, & she had the art of making me feel that her joy was always as fresh and stimulating as the first time: finally, I must confess that during all the time that our commerce together lasted, if my heart was not affected to a certain point, at least I enjoyed a thousand charms, by the infinite agreeableness of her wit, which at every mo-

---

[16]Original footnote: ever in imitation of Nasser and Zulica [two characters in *Vathek, a Comedy in Two Acts*, by Stéphanie Félicité de Genlis].

ment provided her with a thousand new resources; but ultimately I was acknowledged as her lover, and I was indebted to high-society for this homage; there was no reason to expect, being associated with a woman of her type, my being able to conceal an affair & hide it from everyone; I had a thousand eyes fixed on me: I was congratulated, commented on, taunted, informed as regards the thousand disagreeable scenes that befell my predecessors & solicited to deflect from myself all the ridicules I succeeded in bringing on myself: my age, my robe, the indispensable necessity of having someone, & of making a reputation for myself, – didn't save me from any of the nasty jokes or jibes that I was constantly the butt of; but I kept my head above water, I braved the storm, all the talk & repetitions, the couplets, the charitable advice, & my firmness of character allowed for only the excitation of a certain admiration by my enviers, when an unexpected event, although extremely simple in itself, came to appall me, & to put an end to the most absurd, most unbelievable, & most ridiculous sexual passion I have ever enjoyed in all my life.

My sustained goings-on with the duchess had secured for me a consideration that gave me a rather decided authority over her: I had two keys to the hideaway; I held command over it as if I was the owner, & nothing happened there, at least as far as I knew, when I was not a participant: I imagined myself being informed of all the trips that the duchess made there; however, a true friend of mine who had resolved to cure me of a displaced infatuation, assured me so positively to the contrary, & pushed me quite strongly to take a reckoning of it myself; so that I began to have several doubts on certain of the duchess' absences, on certain evenings where the destination was uncertain, which was not normal for a man in my situation: finally we resolved to spy on her; it didn't take long for an opportunity to present itself: two days after I was there at my accustomed hour with the duchess, I was told that she was in bed with a raging migraine, that she was resting, that she was desperate to be deprived of seeing me, that she begged me to pass by the following day in the morning, because she had some things to tell me: I sensed she was pulling a fast one on me, I judged it treachery immediately, & without losing time I went to find my friend who, thrilled by the occasion that had presented itself, dropped everything to accompany me to the hideaway; we arrived quietly, & the keys that I possess allowed me to introduce ourselves without knocking; without hindrance, we reached as far as the antechamber of the room where one hung out ordinarily; without making a sound, we approached the door, where we immediately heard sighs, broken phrases, & certain expressions, which indicated clearly enough the means by which one was *killing time*; I entered brusquely. Judge for yourself our surprise, our reactions, & our attitudes; the duchess was lying on her back half-naked on a couch in the arms of a big lackey we knew, but whose employment we would not have otherwise suspected; their acts and their state of mind was so obvious that there was no means for them to talk their way out of it; my first reaction was, I confess, all that ire can inspire of the most violent kind; & this miserable wretch, who, to mention it in passing, was a large, amusing fellow with a rather pretty face, was so frightened by what he imagined was about to happen to him that without thinking to put his clothes on, which otherwise could only have done him some honor, didn't hesitate to jump brusquely from the balcony into the garden, from which it was easy for him to climb down to the street & make his escape; in a first fit of anger, I chased after him & regaled him with several blows of a stick: but a moment later, realizing that a similar anger could work against me in evil minds, I doubled up with generous laughter, which was for her the culmination of insult.

"Hey, monsieur," she said to me, "what's the point of all this? Am I not the mistress of my own house? What does this authority mean?... that was quite unprecedented...."

It was clear to me that the poor woman was in a pickle despite the superior attitude of her effrontery; so to abridge the conversation, my friend & I, we threw her back down on the bed she had just gotten up from, & there, begging a million apologies of her for having come and bothered her, we treated her a little worse than the least of creatures, that is to say, we made her our plaything and had our way with her, & we did everything to her, except the one thing alone that would have doubtless appeased her. She wanted to assume an air of dignity, to threaten, to employ commonplaces: *"a woman like me... who is fond of the best there is...."* – we didn't respond except by breaking for our entertainment several mantlepiece ornaments, some mirrors, and other like baubles; and we departed by assuring her very respectfully of our obedience, and the great pains we would take that nobody henceforth would be ignorant of the motive and merit of her retreats.

However I wasn't so much the master of my spite as I succeeded in persuading myself, and the first few days that followed this discovery, my sole occupation was to unmask this detestable woman in every corner of Paris & to paint such a hideous portrait of her that the most compromised and discredited man would be completely disgusted to try her; I don't even know to what extent I would have gone in my resentment, when an unexpected adventure came along and destroyed all my plans of vengeance, and opened my eyes to the ridiculousness I had covered myself in, running after the imposing title of abbot à la mode: from this moment on, no more resentment for the duchess, no more desire to replace her by another woman of the same type. There I was at last at the fatal point of my conversion, my dear marquis; at the risk of boring you, I must take a more serious and grave tone now, to enter into the details of a veritable, legitimate passion, & which, against all sorts of appearance, was going to become, in a brief span of time, the happiness of my life.

Part Three: The Triumph of the Nuns

I was invited one day by my uncle, whom I had not stopped cultivating a relationship with, to attend a veil-taking ceremony in an abbey whose abbess was connected to our family. I don't know what presentiment made me receive this offer with a shudder, which seemed to be a precursor to all the events that were about to follow it: I accepted however, & I showed up at my uncle's house at the agreed upon hour: we hastened to be on our way to the abbey where we found a large company of people apparently much disposed to joy as a result of that human inconsequence that takes a kind of pleasure in the sacrifice of a miserable victim, in the sight of someone who is about to be buried alive, – in a word, in a spectacle that ought naturally to communicate the saddest & most lugubrious thoughts; I regarded all these objects with a distracted and inattentive attitude, but all these indifferent reactions soon gave way to everything that was its exact opposite, when I saw the young person in whose honor this ceremony was taking place: Gods, what attractions! What an aggregation of all that nature has ever brought together of the most touching and rare, in one person! A divine waist, the bearing of a queen, a perfectly-shaped face, her eyes!... ah! The eyes of a beautiful woman... at last, dear marquis, I was floored, I was motionless, enraptured, lost in astonishment and love, yes love, no matter what my spiritual brethren say, no matter what our little masters say, no matter what I would have said myself previously; there are moments in life when we are struck by natural attraction, there are connections with faces and organs that strike us, which excite a total upset of the machine on the spot, which are immediately communicated to the heart such as to change the most determined little master's way of thinking: this is incredible, incomprehensible even if one wishes, but that does not make it any less true; I'm a terrible example, I who am speaking, – never has a person pushed intrepidity further in this way than me; I believed exceptionally little in the probity of men, & not at all in the virtue of women: hence the source of my contempt & my scant confidence in & esteem for the two sexes; whatever idea one might have of the change in my way of thinking on so formal an avowal & so poorly concealed internally, I am deeply indifferent to people's comments & judgments, & I confess by the same sincerity which I profess to this day that I experienced interior impulses which were unknown and indefinable to me until then; I immediately fell into the deepest revery that I didn't exit from until the conclusion of a baneful ceremony that pierced my heart: at the fatal moment when the unfortunate victim was deprived of her rich attire in order to be covered by a dark & lugubrious habit, when three or four old veiled harpies declared to her that she must renounce the world and all its pomp; in a word, when they pronounced all this miserable protocol of foolishness, which heedless youth engages in without thinking, which is beyond the human mind's understanding, I emerged as if from the bottom of a tomb; I had been fixing my eyes on her since the beginning of the scene: Heaven! What I went through! What I felt! When I saw her tremble, grow pale, & shed some tears which she made a thousand efforts to hold back: a mortal shiver ran through my veins, my knees buckled beneath me; finally feeling as though I was not in control of my troubled mind or my tears, I stepped away under the pretext of a bloody nose, but in effect suffocating with sadness and despair, & I withdrew to an isolated place to give free rein to the tears that fell in abundance.

However, the accursed ceremony ran its course, & those detestable furies latched on to their prey: my tears had solaced me a little, & I reappeared before the company with a more tranquil composure: it was not difficult for me to give a special color to my absence when nobody had the faintest idea what occasioned it. We returned to Paris, & I affected a gay and dissipated attitude in front of my uncle: I asked him, as if making conversation, who the young lady was that had taken the white veil.

"It is," my uncle responded to me in an indignant tone of voice, "one of the most flagrant examples of parents' injustice & of their blind preventative measures for certain children; the person you just saw is Mademoiselle de P***, daughter of the marchioness of the same name, & quite worthy assuredly of a different fate by the rare advantages of her wit, heart, and face; born of rich parents, endowed with everything that is needed to be adored by them, she has always been the object of their hatred and ill-treatment: a blind penchant, an outrageous preventative measure in favor of their eldest daughter, is the source of this hateful behavior; the latter girl, jealous of all the qualities that shine in her sister, had the harshest and most contemptuous behavior towards her; authorized by her parents, she overwhelmed her by her dishonest behavior, until she finally obtained, about a year ago, that her younger sister should be confined in a convent; the unfortunate Honorine submitted to all this with unfailing gentleness and compliance; she was placed at the abbey we just came from & was commended to the care of the Abbess de Va***, our cousin; I would be unable to furnish you with all the high praise that has been lavished on her by her family on account of her virtue & her sweetness of character; in the end, several months ago, M. the President de S*** asked for her older sister's hand in marriage with his only son, who will be powerfully rich, & her parents by a politic & extremely barbaric and damnable usage, in order to give their eldest daughter a more advantageous dowry, made the unfortunate Honorine to understand that she would have to renounce the world forever; her sweet demeanor, and her obedience, remained constant: she consented to everything & has sustained this terrible blow with a firmness of mind that has made the tears run down my face, & which drew them from everyone else who attended the ceremony.

I was so far from denying myself an emotion that was so called-for and so merited that the tears never stopped running down my face from the beginning of my uncle's recitation: fortunately, night had fallen, & the darkness that reigned in the carriage prevented him from seeing what I had so much interest in hiding: we arrived in Paris, and I went home, where I had nothing more pressing to do than to retire to my room, to abandon myself to the mortal grief that was devouring me. How many bitter reflections I made when I was alone! How many dreadful regrets I had! How many projects were destroyed as soon as they were formed! What a chaos of despairing thoughts! What a terrible future! For in the end, let one call them what they will, – my transports, – I was in love with her, I told myself; I was out of my mind with passion, rage, and despair, & I spent several days in a rather terrible mood, without any possibility of taking control of myself to put some order to all that was occupying my imagination; I learned however that the marriage of the older sister was supposed to take place on the following day: my uncle, who during our visit to the abbey had formed some connections with the family de P***, was asked to give the nuptial benediction for the future spouses; he could not in all honesty refuse, & he sent for me, proposing that I accompany him to the ceremony; I excused myself under the pretext of an indisposition, but in fact I was overcome with grief & rage against this cruel family. The nuptials took place with a splash; I could not avoid *having someone* send a card with my best wishes to their door, but I excused myself from seeing them, & I remained for nearly three months buried in my room, forgetting my fellow man, & absolutely indifferent as to what went on around me.

I was yanked out of my lethargy by a terrible catastrophe that proved to me that, whatever it is that one wished to attribute to a superior order of events, it is always certain that injustice & perversity when carried too far will without fail lead to an impending castigation & an inevitable reversal; the new bride who bore the name of Madame President de S***, in the midst of luxury, splendor, and riches, which seemed to promise her the most happy and brilliant career, took a fall two days later that cost her her life: her father and mother, destroyed by this fatal stroke, & prey to a most terrible despair, followed her to the grave eight days later; so that in two weeks time, the adorable Honorine was removed from the convent, enjoying an immense wealth, & the mistress of her will under the tutelage of the Count de P***, her uncle on the father's side, who had always loved her dearly, & who, completely opposed to the violence that had been exerted prior to this time against his unfortunate niece, vowed to repair all the wrong that had been done to her, while preparing the happiest of futures for her. Such sudden, such unhoped for, changes woke me up out of what seemed like a deep sleep, without knowing precisely what I gained from any of it. A ray of hope presented itself to my heart; I considered it even like a happy presage to me that the Count de P*** had always been an intimate friend of our family: finally, what shall I say, my dear marquis, I reappeared, I *had myself inscribed* at Honorine's uncle's house for a ceremonial visit, & I didn't tarry finding every occasion to accompany my uncle who saw them often. I saw Mademoiselle de P*** again then. Gods! What transports I felt at so cherished a sight; I was trembling and frantic, my embarrassment went so far as to hinder my ability to express myself, & she must have understood precious little of the compliment I paid her: I tried at any rate to fix my eyes on her, she lowered hers, & I believe I saw that she grew red in the face quite a bit; she seemed quite embarrassed for the duration of my visit, & it was easy for me to see that the same embarrassment continued and increased every time I saw her. For me, in the time I set aside to visit her over the course of several months, I discovered so many adorable qualities in Honorine's heart and mind that my love came to the point of exceeding itself and was capable of going to the greatest lengths. I felt that I could not live without having her; but I saw terrible obstacles in my way, impossible to get rid of even for me; I imagined that with her possessing so considerable an estate and so many virtues worthy of admiration by the entire universe, it was impossible that all the most distinguished parties were not fighting over her. In a small amount of time, these crushing ideas produced a visible change in all my exterior: I became dreamy, somber, to the point of being unrecognizable. The Count de P***, who had taken an extreme liking to me, begged me on several occasions to open my heart to him instantly, offering me everything that was in his power to help, with the exception of what alone could have relieved me; Honorine was sometimes present; I didn't answer her uncle's questions except by casting at his niece glances wherein my love and my despair were all too visibly painted: it seemed to me that she was receptive to them, I saw her beautiful eyes grow tender, & on the verge of shedding tears: two or three times even in the middle of a conversation, she brusquely left the room; she was sometimes gone for an entire hour before reappearing, and when she re-entered the room one saw, in spite of herself, always the marks of consternation & despondency on her face: maybe I was exaggerating these things, but I truly loved her, & by consequence I had neither vanity nor confidence; & while supposing even that I should have suspected her of a secret liking for me, how with the habit that I wore, & the eyes that my family had on me, would I have dared to undertake to approach & seduce a girl more respectable even by her virtues than by her brith; my heart was not so corrupt that I could not sense the horror and baseness of such a proceeding; despair then was the only sentiment that I could give myself fully over to, & I do not know to what appalling extremity the excess of an unhappy passion that was hopeless could have taken me, when I learned that my elder brother, to whom the Court had assigned a company of calvary in the regiment of ***, had been killed in the Battle of Lawfeld:[17] an excess of honor and bravery had been the main cause of his downfall; he had just obtained the acceptance of the regiment of ***; he had received his commission the day before battle, and his scrupulousness didn't allow him to abandon it at such a critical moment. The infinite advantages that ac-

---

[17]Battle of Lawfeld: a battle that took place on July 2, 1747, during the War of Austrian Succession, between the French and a combined force of Austrian, German, Dutch, and British troops.

crued to me on this loss were incapable of consoling me; with him I had lost a most tender brother & the most perfect friend; he was widely missed as an excellent subject of the crown & someone who would have one day become a great officer.

Everyone could see that his loss caused a change in my situation; the little collar was refashioned, & I became the sole inheritor of my house; soon even the topic of marriage was brought up to me: I asked for nothing better; I seized this opportunity to introduce my uncle to my secret: he praised me highly for my choice & took it upon himself to sound out the Count de P***, who was an intimate friend of his. His proposition was received with joy, & a few days later I was presented to Mademoiselle de P*** as someone who was to be her spouse. She received me blushing, but I did not see in her eyes any anger, nor indifference. I easily found the occasion to speak with her without witnesses present, & it was then that this virtuous girl, feeling authorized enough by the count's consent, ingenuously confessed to me that her inclination had followed closely in line with what she had noticed to be my own, and that the unlikely appearance of her wishes coming true had cost her as many tears as it did me. Gods, what pleasure! What extreme delight filled my heart on hearing so charming a confession! Only people who have truly loved can understand it; I didn't waste a moment in engaging my uncle to bring the matter to a conclusion: he is the absolute master in my family: his will is law: thus, in no time, all the proper arrangements were made, the two houses viewing this alliance with infinite joy:

we are to be united, finally, in several days time & we are only waiting for the arrangement of some small family affairs, & the return of Honorine who has gone to the countryside with her uncle in order to visit some relatives who live there. The purpose of her trip was to hasten our union & to accelerate the most fortunate moment of our lives.

And there you have it, my dear marquis, what you asked me for with such eagerness, what I promised to give you with pleasure, & what I have taken so much trouble and made so much effort to keep for you, & this on account of my not imagining that it could ever have been brought to a conclusion: it's a sketch, not at all refined, in broad strokes, from page to page finally, without knowing precisely how I have succeeded in bringing it to a close; & provided that I have amused you & satisfied you, I am extremely glad. Only one thing is missing, and that is the pleasure to see again, safe and sound, & to embrace, the best and tenderest of all my friends.

FIN

Other Books by the Publisher

Fanchette's Pretty Little Foot
by Restif de La Bretonne

Je M'Accuse...
by Léon Bloy

My Hospitals & My Prisons
by Paul Verlaine

Salvation Through the Jews
by Léon Bloy

Words of a Demolitions Contractor
by Léon Bloy

Cellulely
by Paul Verlaine